"YOU HAVE TO STAND THIS CLOSE, BILLIE, or you won't be able to follow my lead." Cord said.

His breath fanned her cheek as he spoke. It was the first time he'd said her name, and she liked how it sounded on his tongue. He began to move to the music, and she tried to follow.

"Relax, Billie, close your eyes and think only of the music."

She tried to do what he said, but it wasn't easy to concentrate. Every nerve in her body stood at attention. Then the music stopped and so did they. She raised her head and their gazes locked and held for what seemed an eternity.

The look in his eyes said it all. He was going to kiss her.

His grip tightened, molding her soft curves to his body. A faint light flickered in the depths of his black eyes. "I've never kissed a doctor before."

"I've never kissed a rogue," she confessed.

"We're even, then." The last word was smothered on her lips as his mouth captured hers. . . .

WHAT ARE *LOVESWEPT* ROMANCES?

They are stories of true romance and touching emotion. We believe those two very important ingredients are constants in our highly sensual and very believable stories in the LOVESWEPT line. Our goal is to give you, the reader, stories of consistently high quality that may sometimes make you laugh, sometimes make you cry, but are always fresh and creative and contain many delightful surprises within their pages.

Most romance fans read an enormous number of books. Those they truly love, they keep. Others may be traded with friends and soon forgotten. We hope that each LOVESWEPT romance will be a treasure—a "keeper." We will always try to publish

LOVE STORIES YOU'LL NEVER FORGET
BY AUTHORS YOU'LL ALWAYS REMEMBER

The Editors

KISSED BY A ROGUE

CHARLOTTE HUGHES

BANTAM BOOKS
NEW YORK · TORONTO · LONDON · SYDNEY · AUCKLAND

KISSED BY A ROGUE

A Bantam Book / December 1993

*LOVESWEPT and the wave design are registered
trademarks of Bantam Books, a division of
Bantam Doubleday Dell Publishing Group, Inc.
Registered in U.S. Patent
and Trademark Office and elsewhere.*

If you would be interested in receiving protective vinyl covers for your
Loveswept books, please write to this address for information:

Loveswept
Bantam Books
P.O. Box 985
Hicksville, NY 11802

ISBN 0-553-44389-5

Published simultaneously in the United States and Canada

Bantam Books are published by Bantam Books, a division of Bantam Doubleday Dell Publishing Group, Inc. Its trademark, consisting of the words
"Bantam Books" and the portrayal of a rooster, is Registered in U.S. Patent
and Trademark Office and in other countries. Marca Registrada. Bantam
Books, 1540 Broadway, New York, New York 10036.

PRINTED IN THE UNITED STATES OF AMERICA

OPM   0 9 8 7 6 5 4 3 2 1

For Lois Walker with love.

This Dr. was not the most dynamic of heroines. Her chosen profession seems like it would call for a stronger minded person.

The relationship was to strong to quick. No gradual build-up.

Liked the mystery aspect of this book.

The rest of it .... Ho Hum!

Many thanks to Dr. Ellores Brailey,
Karla Racer, and Russell A. White
for assisting me with research.

ONE

WELCOME TO HELL.

Billie Foster gazed tiredly at the road sign where the WELCOME TO RUCKERS had been crossed out with garish green paint and the letters H-E-L-L substituted. Beneath it, the population had been altered from 4,908 to 4,907. Smart person, she thought, as she followed the narrow, twisting road and entered the town—or what there was of it. So far all she'd seen was swampland.

The clinic was a sprawling one-story structure tucked between Jones's Mortuary and a gas station offering a twenty-four-hour towing service. All three buildings were in dire need of painting. Billie sighed as she parked along the street and regarded the town that was to be her home for the next couple of years. This was why she'd spent the past twelve years in college and medical school. This was why her father had worked two jobs, why her mother had cleaned other people's houses, and why Billie herself had struggled to maintain scholarship grades and work part time as well. When the money had run out, she'd taken out a government loan. A desperate act, but she would have borrowed from the KGB at that point. She was the first Foster ever to graduate college, much less medical school. As Billie ran a brush through her dark hair and made minor repairs to her makeup, she was thankful no one in her family was there to witness her disappointment.

It was time to repay Uncle Sam.

Nurse Naomi Bradshaw looked as though she had been stuffed into the white polyester jumpsuit that was her uniform. As she gazed at Billie through horn-rimmed glasses that clashed with her teased red-orange hair, she didn't bother to hide her dismay.

"*You're* Dr. Billie Foster" she said. "But you're a woman!" She made it sound like an incurable disease. "Does Dr. Barnaby know?" she asked, then went on before Billie could answer. "No, he couldn't possibly know. He would have said something to me."

Billie shifted uncomfortably as the woman scrutinized her with the same painstaking thoroughness one might employ in studying a new strain of influenza. "Where *is* Dr. Barnaby, by the way?" Billie asked, shrugging her shoulders, trying to work out the soreness from her having spent so many hours in a compact car designed for practicality instead of comfort.

"Fishing. Dr. B. always goes fishing on Monday."

"Who takes care of the patients?"

"Patients don't come in on Dr. B.'s fishing day." The woman said it matter-of-factly and with a finality that suggested fishing on Monday carried as much weight as the Commandment that ordered rest on Sunday.

Billie nodded as though it made complete sense. "I know this is going to sound like a dumb question, but what happens if there's an emergency?"

"Shorty Robbins over at the fire department handles 'em. He's our paramedic."

"I see." Billie glanced around the empty waiting room where a black-and-white TV was tuned in to the Oprah Winfrey Show. Finally, she regarded the nurse with another smile. "Perhaps you could give me directions to the house where I'll be staying," she said. "I'd like to get cleaned up."

"Come with me." Nurse Bradshaw stood and motioned for Billie to follow. Her shoes created sucking noises against the linoleum floor, and her thighs rubbed together with each step she took. She led Billie to the back of the building and opened a door. "That's it."

Billie's heart sank at the sight of the two-story building. "It looks like a garage."

"It is. We used to keep the ambulance there before Shorty came along. There's an apartment upstairs. Nothing fancy, but it keeps the cold out in winter and the mosquitoes out in summer." She paused and stuck her pencil in her hair where several others, long forgotten, jutted out in all directions. "The refrigerator is stocked. Once folks found out you was on your way, they got busy baking. You got a pretty view from your back porch. The Suwannee River runs almost to your back steps."

"That's nice," Billie said, trying to muster up a little enthusiasm over that fact.

"Why don't you run on over and have a look at it? I'll give you a call if something comes up. Nothing will, of course, with it being Monday. Anyway, we close in an hour."

"Who's on call tonight?"

"Dr. B. will take the calls until he has a chance to show you around. He said it was a shame you had to come in on his fishing day. 'Course, that was before he knew you was a woman. I don't know what he'll have to say to that."

"Tell him to take it up with the United States government," Billie muttered on her way out. "He's stuck with me for the next two years whether he likes it or not."

Several minutes later Billie found herself staring

in dismay at the tiny three-room apartment that was to be her home. The furniture was a mismatched collection of overstuffed pieces with faded floral covers and old rattan. She shook her head sadly, thinking of the many ratty apartments she'd lived in over the years in order to afford her education. One day, she would look back and laugh. One day, when she could afford a nice place of her own, when she could repay her parents for all their hard work and love, when she could buy a new dress and not have to feel guilty over it.

She hoped she wouldn't have to wait much longer for that day.

Billie wasn't certain at what point the old air conditioner in her bedroom died. She awoke late in the night to an oppressive heat, her pajamas clinging to her damp body. She flipped on her lamp and tried to figure out what had happened to the old window unit, but she could have been examining the engine of a Boeing 747 for all she knew. She didn't have a mechanical bone in her body.

Twenty minutes later Billie had managed to pry open only one window in the entire apartment. The others had obviously been painted closed. Sweat trickled between her breasts. She grabbed a soft drink from the refrigerator, unlocked her door, and stepped out into the night air.

The moon was full, turning the narrow ribbon of water behind her apartment silver. A light breeze fluttered the leaves of a giant elm, cooling Billie's flushed cheeks and bringing with it the scent of gardenia. She sat on the top step for a long time listening to the chortle of crickets. Off in the distance she thought she heard a woman's laughter.

Billie left the steps a moment later and sighed her immense pleasure when her toes sank into the lush, cool grass. She walked closer to the river, thankful for the bright moon that lit her way. As a child, she had loved the outdoors, frolicking about with her brother, who'd taught her to swim and climb trees and arm-wrestle with the best of them. That was before high school, before Billie had decided to become a doctor. The need for scholarship grades had left her little time for the outdoors or anything else.

Billie came to an abrupt halt when she heard the laughter again, a high-pitched lilting sound, this time followed by a masculine chuckle. Intrigued, Billie moved in the direction of the sounds, picking her way carefully across the loamy riverbank.

She saw them a moment later, standing on the other side of the water. The woman was tall and blond, hair falling in massive curls down her back. She moved like something in a fairy tale. The man was cloaked in shadows. Billie inched closer.

She was no more than fifty feet from them when

she realized the woman was naked. Billie took a step back, suddenly realizing she had come upon two skinny-dippers. She turned to go, just as the man stepped out of the shadows.

He was nothing like anyone she'd ever seen before, tall and straight as the towering pines that skirted the beach. He was massive and powerfully built, his naked flesh the color of Brazil nuts. Standing on the other side of the river, Billie got an undistorted view of his wide, hair-roughened chest, flat stomach, and muscular thighs. She felt her cheeks burn as her gaze found the juncture between his legs where a thatch of black hair nestled around his sex. He was aroused. She sucked her breath in sharply at the sight.

Billie took another step back. It was obvious what the man had on his mind by the way he watched the woman. In another five minutes they'd be making love. She had absolutely no business being there. Nevertheless, she found herself captivated by his dark beauty. She tried to convince herself her perusal was strictly professional and based on the fact that she had seen so many neglected bodies that she couldn't help but appreciate one as fine as this. Whom was she kidding? There wasn't a professional thought in her head at the moment. She had grown warm and achy just looking at him.

Something moved in the bush in front of her, and Billie froze. Probably just a squirrel, she told herself. But as it skittered out, it landed on top of one bare foot. She cried out, and the sound shattered the silence. She took a step back, lost her balance, and fell with the grace of a pregnant hippo into a thorny bush of wild blackberries.

On the other side of the river, the man snapped his head up. Despite her attempts to hide, Billie knew her white cotton pajamas stood out like a beacon. She scrambled to her feet and ran.

She didn't stop running until she reached the safety of her apartment. She bolted the door, then leaned against it and tried to catch her breath. What had come over her? She had almost watched two perfect strangers make love. It was sometime later when she finally climbed into bed and tried to go to sleep.

TWO

Dr. Eustace Barnaby peered at the petite brunette through wire-framed spectacles, studying her with the same enthusiasm he might a bad case of black spot on his beloved rosebushes. "So you're the new doctor." His tone was flat as unrisen dough.

Billie gave him her best smile and held out her hand. "Billie Foster," she said.

The old doctor gave a snort and went back to writing something on a patient's chart, ignoring her outstretched hand altogether. "You don't look old enough to have graduated high school, much less medical school. And nobody said anything about you being a woman."

Billie crossed her arms and regarded the wiry white-haired man who seemed so intent on disliking her. He wasn't going to make it easy. "I'm twenty-eight years old," she said, always amazed that anyone thought she looked younger. Four years of residency at a busy hospital had left her little time to pamper herself. "I'm sure the information is in my records," she added.

"Well, if you think you're going to waltz into *my* clinic and treat *my* patients as if they're your own, you're wrong."

It was Billie's understanding that she was to do *exactly* that. The old doctor was well past retirement age, and the townspeople were desperate for a new physician. At least that's what she had been told. Now, Dr. Barnaby was telling her something entirely different. "Then perhaps you should tell me why I'm here," she said at last.

He looked at her long and hard. "I haven't the foggiest idea," he said. He walked out of the room and slammed the door behind him.

Billie examined the woman before her and shook her head sadly at the sight. "Mrs. Miller, I *do* believe this is the worst case of poison ivy I've ever seen. How long have you been this way?"

The woman on the examining table blinked through red swollen eyes. "Couple of weeks. My husband and I started clearing our lot weekend before last. We plan to start building a house soon." She paused and gazed at the welts on her skin. "I don't understand it, Dr. Foster. I've been so careful to wear long sleeves and gloves. I can't imagine how I'm getting infected."

Billie nodded sympathetically. "I'll give you an injection that should stop the itching right away," she said, scribbling on the woman's chart as she spoke. "I'll also write you a prescription for something. Just follow the instructions and—" Billie was interrupted by a sharp knock on the door. Dr. Barnaby peeked his head through and grinned at the woman on the examining table.

"I heard we had a bad case of poison ivy in room one," he said.

Mrs. Miller smiled at the old doctor and displayed both arms so he could see for himself. "Believe me, Doc, it's bad."

Dr. Barnaby stepped inside and closed the door behind him. "Cara, aren't you and Ben a little mature to be sneaking off into the woods?"

The woman blushed. "We've been clearing our lot."

He drew his thick brows into a thoughtful frown. "Wearing gloves, are you?"

She nodded. "Not to mention long sleeves and long pants."

"And what are you doing with all that you clear?"

"Burning it."

"Well, there you are."

Billie, who'd been quiet up until that moment, stepped closer. "You mean she's getting infected from the smoke?"

"Why'd you think her eyes are so puffy, *Doctor*?" he said, making the word sound like one of those four-letter ones often found on bathroom walls. "Or did you miss that in your examination?" He turned to Billie and all but snatched the prescription pad out of her hand. "What are you giving her? Oh, cripes, you don't want to give her that." He ripped the sheet off the pad, wadded it up, and tossed it in the trash.

Billie stared back at him in disbelief.

"How do you expect Cara and her husband to build their new house if they've got medical bills to pay?" he demanded. He didn't wait for her response. Instead, he turned to the patient. "You'll have to forgive Dr. Foster here," he said. "She's used to doing things by the book." He rolled his eyes heavenward as though he couldn't believe his misfortune to have ended up with such a nitwit in his clinic.

Billie was genuinely offended but decided not to say anything in front of the patient. "What do you suggest, Dr. Barnaby?" she asked in a professional tone.

"Table salt."

"Table salt?"

"That's right." He turned to Mrs. Miller. "I want you to take several baths a day with plain old table salt, Cara. Just dump that salt in the tub while the water's running and mix it up. Then, when you get out, I want you to rub down with petroleum jelly.

It'll make a mess of your sheets, but I promise you won't itch. That salt kills the poison every time."

"Thanks, Doc," the woman said, obviously in a hurry to get home and do just that.

Billie waited until Mrs. Miller left the room before saying anything to the old doctor. "May I have a word with you?" she said, before he could leave as well.

"Make it a fast word. I've got patients."

"You had no right to walk into this room in the middle of my examination and change all my instructions."

Two bushy brows shot up high on the old doctor's forehead. "I'm the physician in charge, and I can do what I dang well please. Besides, you don't know anything about real doctorin'. Everything you know came straight out of a textbook."

"I spent my residency at Richmond General," she replied. "One of the biggest hospitals in the state of Virginia, not to mention the best trauma unit. I think that should count for something."

"This ain't Richmond," he said, "and most of the folks in these parts are simple mill people. They can't afford all these fancy medicines. Not when there's something cheaper to be had." He paused for breath.

"Back when I started practicing, folks had less money than they do now. I can't tell you how many times I've gone home with a sack of turnips for treating a bad cold. I delivered a baby once and was given a hunting dog in exchange."

Billie knew there was no reasoning with the old doctor. "I'm not sure what the AMA would think of your tactics, but I'm always willing to learn. Just don't expect me to cure everything with sugar water and rabbit tobacco."

The banging noise woke her.

Billie rolled over in her bed and blinked against the darkness. On a chair nearby, her new rotating fan created just enough cool air to make the room tolerable. She raised up, glanced at her alarm clock, and saw that it was almost two o'clock in the morning. Then, the banging started again. Someone was pounding on her door. She jumped from the bed and groped for a light switch.

Thirty seconds later Billie snatched up the shade over her door and found herself looking into a blond woman's face. She looked vaguely familiar, but Billie didn't have time to stop and think where she'd seen her.

"Are you the new doctor?" the woman called out from the other side of the small window.

Billie unlocked the door and dragged it open. "What's wrong?"

"My friend has been injured. Someone broke a whiskey bottle over his head. He's bleeding bad."

"Did you call Dr. Barnaby?"

"There wasn't time. We were down the street when it happened, so I drove straight to the clinic."

Billie grabbed a key hanging next to the door. "Can you get your friend inside the waiting room?"

The woman's expression was doubtful. "I can try."

"I'll be there in two minutes."

With no time to waste, Billie raced into her bedroom and grabbed the first thing she could find, a pair of cutoffs and an old college T-shirt. She would pull on a lab coat at the clinic. She stuffed her feet into worn sneakers and took off, trying to comb her hair with her fingers as she went. She hurried out the door and down the flight of stairs. A moment later she was switching lights on in the clinic. She opened the front door, then froze at the sight of the woman trying to help the injured man up the steps. Seeing them together, she recognized them immediately as the man and woman from the river. Billie stood there several seconds, remembering how she had watched them through the trees. Her cheeks flamed at the memory.

"Son of a bitch! I'm bleeding like a stuck pig."

Billie jumped at the sound of his voice. He had looked powerful on the riverbank, but nothing could have prepared her for this close-up version. He carried himself with a commanding air of self-confidence even as blood spurted from his forehead.

"Stop yelling, honeykins," the woman told him, trying to hold a towel against his injury. "You'll wake the whole neighborhood!"

Billie snapped into action at the sight of his gaping wound, irritated with herself for letting her emotions get in the way. The man could bleed to death while she was gawking at him as if she were a hormone-rabid schoolgirl. "Come this way, please," she said, at last sounding like the professional she was supposed to be.

"Who are you?" The man had stopped cussing long enough to appear curious.

Billie met his gaze and wondered how she had known his eyes would be the color of charcoal. His hair gleamed blue-black under the fluorescent lights. The shadow of a beard gave him a slightly rakish look. He smelled of whiskey. "I'm Dr. Foster," she said. "We need to get you to the back." The man did his share of muttering and cussing but followed nevertheless.

"Tell me what happened," Billie said, as soon as they reached the examining room. The man continued to rant and rave about getting revenge on the person responsible for his injury. Billie didn't miss the dangerous look in his eyes, and she was thankful she hadn't landed the offensive blow.

The blonde didn't waste any time explaining. "We were having a nice quiet drink at the Cypress Lounge when a couple of roughnecks got into a fight over what they wanted to hear on the jukebox. The whole place went wild. We were almost out the door when somebody smashed a bottle over his head."

"Help me get him onto the examining table," Billie said, then discovered it was no easy task. He was well over six feet and had to weigh close to two hundred pounds. Finally, they succeeded.

The man regarded Billie curiously, his eyes taking in her mussed hair, the pink flush on her cheeks. It was obvious he had gotten her out of bed. "You don't look like any doctor I ever met," he said, noting the shorts and T-shirt.

Billie met his look. He was staring. She realized then that she had forgotten to put on a lab coat. The T-shirt was thin from so many washings, and her nipples had hardened the minute she stepped inside the cold room. Billie reached for one of the coats hanging on the door and pulled it on quickly.

"Do I know you?" he asked.

She paused briefly. Once again, she could feel color staining her cheeks. "No, we haven't met. Now, please you're going to have to sit still." She reached for the cloth at his head and pulled it away so she could get a look at his wound. The hairline gash was deep.

"Oh my God!" The blonde looked as though she might faint. "I think I'll wait out front." She was out the door in a split second.

The man chuckled. "It must be bad."

Billie cleaned the wound. "Not too bad. I just don't think your friend cares much for the sight of blood."

"She's not my friend. She's my father's mistress."

Billie glanced up. "I see."

His look was penetrating. "Yeah, I'll bet you do."

"You're going to need stitches, Mr.—"

"No."

"The cut is fairly deep and—"

He shook his head. "I don't have time for that. I'm in a hurry."

"Yes, of course," she said tightly. "There must be one or two more beer joints open at this hour." She had no right to scold him, of course, but she was irritated. He had dragged her out of bed at this ungodly hour, and now he wasn't cooperating.

The dark scowl disappeared for a moment, and he looked amused. "What kind of doctor are you?"

"I'm a general practitioner."

"You planning on being around for a while?"

"Long enough to treat your wound," she said, being deliberately vague. Another day like the one she'd spent with Dr. Barnaby, and there was no telling *what* she'd do. "Now, about those stitches." They argued for a few minutes. Finally, she gave up. A butterfly bandage would probably do the trick. She started to work. His skin was hot, despite the coolness of the room. He watched every move she made, those black eyes curious and alert. It was the most uncomfortable five minutes of her life, and Billie didn't breathe freely until she stepped away to wash her hands at the sink. Still she could feel him watching her.

"I've closed the wound with a butterfly dressing," she said. "I'm sending you home with gauze and instructions on how to keep it clean. I suggest you call Dr. Barnaby in a couple of days to check it."

"I'd rather call you."

Billie almost dropped the envelope of gauze. He was flirting with her. She ignored him. "I need some information before you go."

"What kind of information?"

"Name, address, phone number."

"You planning on calling me for a date?" The look she shot him made him grin. "Look, I'm sorry I gave you such a hard time. It's just . . . I don't much care for doctors."

"Then we're even. I don't much care for men who fight in beer joints."

He chuckled, slid off the table in one fluid movement and approached her. "You know, for a little thing like yourself, you sure are full of spirit."

He was uncomfortably close again. But there was a difference now that he wasn't sitting on the table waiting for her to take care of his wound. She was reminded how big he was, a good ten or twelve inches taller than her own five-foot-two frame. The examining room seemed to shrink in size. Billie took a step back, and her hips made contact with the cabinet behind her. There was no escape. "You can fill this out in the waiting room," she said, handing him a clipboard of patient-information forms. She desperately wanted to put some space between them.

He took the clipboard and laid it on the counter behind her. His arm brushed hers as he did so, and Billie felt a tingle clear down to her wrist. He reached into his back pocket for his wallet. "This should take care of my expenses," he said, tossing a hundred-dollar bill onto the counter. Billie stared back wordlessly, conscious of every nuance. Suddenly, there didn't seem to be enough air in her lungs. She took a deep, shuddering breath, and the sound seemed to echo off the walls. He smiled as though he found her discomfort amusing; then, before she knew it, he lowered his head and touched her lips with his own. Her heart skipped a beat.

Finally, he broke the kiss. "Thanks, Doc. I'm much obliged."

Billie was too shaken to follow. She felt as though her entire nervous system had been short-circuited. She heard him wake the woman in the next room, heard them leave through the front door. Trembling from head to foot, Billie turned off the lights and locked up. She could still taste his kiss when she climbed into bed a few minutes later.

Then it hit her; she didn't have the first clue who he was.

THREE

"What d'you mean you didn't get his name?" Dr. Barnaby asked, when Billie told him about the small emergency during the night.

"I asked him twice. What was I supposed to do, arm-wrestle the information out of him?"

"Why wasn't I called?"

"There wasn't time. He was bleeding all over the place."

"So you stitched him up and let him go!"

"He refused stitches. I used a butterfly dressing instead."

The old doctor's face grew red. "Did it cross your mind to take an X ray?"

"It crossed my mind, but I didn't feel it necessary. And I knew you'd have a fit if I charged one of your patients for something he didn't really need."

He regarded her matter-of-factly. "You realize we could have a lawsuit on our hands."

Billie stared back at him for a moment. Instinct told her the old doctor wouldn't have been satisfied no matter what she'd done for the patient. It didn't matter that she had spent a good portion of her residency working in an emergency room where gunshot wounds and automobile accidents had been the norm, where she had been forced to make life-and-death decisions routinely. This was simply no big deal. "Someone broke a whiskey bottle over his head," she said, trying to sound calm and professional. "It was a superficial wound. He was alert and experiencing no problems with his vision. I did not suspect a concussion."

"But you don't know that for a fact. Not without an X ray."

Billie was half afraid the veins on the old doctor's forehead would pop in his agitation. "What do you expect me to do, Dr. Barnaby?"

"Find him. Bring him back so I can check him thoroughly. The way you should have checked him in the first place."

"How do you suggest I find him when I don't even know his name, for pete's sake?"

"That's your problem, Doctor."

Billie watched him walk out. She'd never felt more confused or frustrated in her life. She couldn't do a damn thing right as far as the old doctor was concerned. She sighed heavily, just as Nurse Bradshaw came through the door.

"I couldn't help overhearing," she said.

"I'm sure the entire waiting room heard." Billie was determined not to let the old man win every battle. He wasn't the first difficult physician she'd had to deal with. "How am I supposed to find a man when I don't know his name or address?" she said.

Nurse Bradshaw stepped closer. "Try the mill. Buford Textiles. Half the people in town work there. That'd be your best bet."

Buford Textiles sat on the edge of town, a sprawling three-story structure that manufactured various fabrics and provided hundreds of jobs. Billie was impressed, not only with its size but with the way it was maintained. She had expected the worst, a ramshackle building with inadequate facilities and poor working conditions. This mill, with its freshly painted exterior and perfectly manicured grounds, was anything but. A security guard at the main gate issued her a visitor's pass and pointed her in the direction of the administrative offices.

"Our personnel manager is on vacation," a smartly dressed receptionist told Billie. "Our plant manager will see you instead."

Bill Crenshaw, a gray-haired man in a seersucker suit, greeted Billie warmly and acted as though he had all the time in the world to give her.

"I heard we had a new doctor in town," he said,

once he'd led her into his office and insisted she have a cup of coffee. "I'll have to admit you're much easier on the eyes than Doc Barnaby. Now what can I do for you?"

Billie told him about the man she'd treated the night before, stating only that it had been a simple head wound. She left out the part that he'd smelled of whiskey and had sustained the injury in a barroom brawl. The last thing she wanted to do was get anybody fired, if the man indeed worked there. "He left before I could get his name," she added. "I don't think he's in any danger, but Dr. Barnaby wants to have a look at him just in case."

"What's he look like?"

"Tall. Close to six-and-a-half feet. Black hair and eyes." It was an accurate description but did not take into account some of the man's finer traits—the broad shoulders, his massive chest, those powerful thighs. But she couldn't very well tell Bill Crenshaw how the stranger's shirt had strained against that same chest, how his snug denims had enticed her, the way his very presence had filled the room and made her forget professional decorum for a fleeting moment. And she certainly couldn't tell him about the kiss and the fact that she'd seen him stark naked only twenty-four hours before. "His forehead will be bandaged," she said instead.

Bill Crenshaw made note of the description on a legal pad. "I'll be sure to keep an eye out," he promised, then paused and looked worried. "He's not in any trouble, is he?"

"Oh, no. We just want to get more information for our files."

He looked relieved. "This is a family-owned operation," he said, "and we keep our standards high. We don't hire riffraff." He swallowed the last of his coffee and offered her another cup.

Billie declined. "I need to get back to the clinic," she said, deciding Dr. Barnaby would have had time to change the locks on the doors by now. He would be none too pleased to learn she was no closer to discovering the phantom patient's identity. She stood. "I appreciate your seeing me."

He stood as well. "Don't mention it. I'm sorry I can't help you, but I'll be sure to mention it to the supervisors out in the mill and ask them to check around. In the meantime you tell Doc Barnaby I said to take good care of you. This town needs a new doctor."

Billie smiled and thanked him. It was nice to see a friendly face. "I'll be sure to tell him," she promised.

Billie was still smiling when she hurried out of the building a moment later. She felt more optimistic now that she'd met someone who didn't begrudge the fact she was there. Perhaps there was hope yet. She started for the parking area, then paused as a black Corvette sped past her. She couldn't help wondering what textile workers were paid these days for one to be able to afford such a car. Perhaps she had made the wrong career choice, she thought as she unlocked the door to her own clunker and climbed in. She rolled the window down, slipped her key into the ignition, then jumped, startled half out of her wits as someone leaned inside her window. Her hand flew to her chest as though she were half-afraid her heart might leap out and fly away.

It was him!

"Well, well, if it ain't the pretty new doctor. Sorry I scared you, Doc," he added with a grin. "People who scare that easily usually have a guilty conscience."

This time he was clean-shaven and smelled of soap and after-shave. His black hair was damp and combed straight back to accommodate the neat white bandage on his forehead. "I've been looking for you," Billie told him. "You left last night before I could get your name and address."

He smiled boldly, showing teeth that were as perfect and symmetrical as the rest of his face. "Afraid I wouldn't call you, huh? Don't worry, I was giving you time to get settled in before I asked you out. I didn't want to appear overly anxious."

Billie gave an exasperated sigh. He really was an arrogant so-and-so. "Look, I don't have time for games, Mr.—"

"My friends call me Cord. What do I call you?"

"Dr. Foster will do perfectly fine." That drew an amused smile from him. "Dr. Barnaby wants to see you in the office right away," she said. "He's concerned that I didn't take an X ray last night."

"Giving you a hard time, is he?"

"I didn't say that."

"He must be. Otherwise, you wouldn't have run out here looking for me." He paused. "Or maybe it doesn't have anything to do with the old doc after all. Could be you liked that kiss so much, you decided to come back for more. Could be you liked what you saw on the riverbank and—"

Her face flamed. She turned on the ignition. "I don't know what you're talking about."

He leaned closer, and his gaze was so intense, it startled her. "That was you on the riverbank the other night." He continued to stare, and when he spoke again, his voice had dropped a pitch. "How come you left in such a hurry?" he asked. "I was just warming up to the idea of being watched."

Billie could feel the blush racing up her neck and staining her cheeks. She slammed her car into reverse with trembling hands. "You're way out of line, mister," she said. "I don't care if your brains fall out of that hole in your head, I'm just doing my job. I would appreciate it if you'd deal with Dr. Barnaby from now on."

"Why don't I come in around lunchtime and have the old doc check me?" he suggested, obviously unaffected by her anger. "Then you and I can grab a bite to eat afterward."

Billie almost laughed out loud at the invitation. "You must be out of your mind."

He chuckled. "That's a known fact," he said. "But I'm still offering to take you to lunch. You could do worse than me, you know."

"I'd have to comb every beer joint in this town to find that out, though, wouldn't I?"

He grinned. His smile was pure deviltry. "You don't like me worth a cuss, do you?"

"You're right. And if I'd known you were so arrogant, I wouldn't have tried so hard to protect your job back there."

"Protect my job?"

"I didn't tell the plant manager how drunk you were when you came into the clinic last night, nor did I tell him you'd been in a fight."

He shrugged. "All the more reason to buy you lunch."

"I'd sooner eat with an earthworm." With that, she rolled up her window and backed out of the parking slot. She drove away, hoping she'd seen the last of him.

"Why in tarnation didn't you tell me our head wound was Cordell Buford?" Dr. Barnaby demanded shortly before noon that same day.

Billie, who'd just spent the past twenty minutes treating an irate nine-month-old for an ear infection, gave the old doctor a blank look. "I beg your pardon?"

"The man who came in here last night," he said. "Do you have any idea who he is?"

"Obviously not."

"Cordell Buford of Buford Textiles. His daddy owns a half-dozen mills throughout the Southeast. Not to mention this town."

"How can someone own a town?" Billie asked, remembering how she had worried about jeopardizing Cordell Buford's job. He was probably having a good laugh over it right now.

"I hope you were nice to him," Dr. Barnaby said, ignoring her question. "He's waiting for you in room two."

"Me?" She shook her head. "Oh, no, you don't. You're not sticking me with that man. Besides, I have a patient with a sore throat waiting in room four."

"I'll take the sore throat, you take Cordell Buford. He specifically asked for you. We try to give the Bufords what they want."

"Why?" she demanded, fighting the impulse to stamp her feet.

"Because without them we wouldn't have a clinic," he said matter-of-factly. He left her before she could argue further.

Billie entered the examining room a few minutes

later and found Cord Buford sitting on the table reading a magazine. "Afternoon, Dr. Foster," he said, giving her a smile.

"Good afternoon, Mr. Buford," she said, turning on her professional voice. She would not give him the satisfaction of knowing how uncomfortable she was. Not to mention embarrassed at mistaking him for a mill worker when he, in fact, owned the damn thing as well as a respectable number of others. As if that weren't enough to embarrass the daylights out of her, there was still the fact that he knew she had watched him from the riverbank that night. But she was determined to get through the exam without adding to her ever-growing list of humiliations. "How does your head feel?" she asked in an impersonal, no-nonsense voice that suggested she had no time for idle chitchat.

"As if somebody hit me over the head with a whiskey bottle," he said. "Look, is this going to take long? I'm supposed to meet someone for lunch."

Billie looked up from his chart, only to find him checking his wristwatch as if he were in a great hurry, as if he were doing her a favor by being there. How had he managed to turn the tables on her, to put her on the defensive? And what was this business about lunch? Was he so unaccustomed to being turned down that he thought she'd change her mind and go after all? "I said no to lunch," she reminded him.

He shrugged. "So I asked someone else." He

paused. "Why—did you change your mind?" The confident tone suggested he would not be at all surprised if she had.

The man was insufferable. Billie gave him a look that would have chilled the furnaces of hell. "No, I didn't change my mind. As for your other question, I don't plan to spend any more time with you than absolutely necessary." He grinned in response, and Billie didn't miss the satisfied look in his eyes. He had succeeded in goading her to the point of anger. She could pretend indifference as long as she liked, but he knew he was getting under her skin.

She smiled back, benevolently. Darned if she wasn't determined to beat him at his own game.

"I'm sure you have important business to attend to," she said, sarcasm slipping into her voice. "Now that the local bars have opened for the day." She heard him chuckle as she turned to the sink and washed her hands. She took longer than necessary both anticipating and dreading the moment when she would have to remove the bandage. Touch him. "All I want to do is clean your wound so Dr. Barnaby can have a look. You haven't experienced any dizziness or blurred vision, have you?" She dried her hands on a paper towel, turned, and found him staring at her legs.

"My vision is just fine, Doc."

There was a knock at the door, and Dr. Barnaby stepped in. Billie had never been so happy to see

him. This was one patient she was only too glad to
hand over to his care. At the same time she witnessed
a drastic change in the old doctor.

"Cord, my boy!" he said, greeting him as though
he were a long-lost son. "How are you?" He took the
younger man's hand and pumped it enthusiastically.
He checked the wound on Cord's forehead. "I heard
you were in an accident. Don't tell me some jealous
husband finally got a hold of you." He gave the
younger man a hearty wink.

Cord looked slightly embarrassed. "Now you
know I don't run with married women, Doc," he said.
"You'll have Dr. Foster thinking the worst of me." He
winced as Dr. Barnaby probed his wound. "Truth is,
after last night, I've decided to give up the fast life."

Dr. Barnaby paused and looked impressed. "No
kidding?"

"That's right. I'm finished with sowin' my wild
oats, Doc. Getting too old for it, if you want the
truth."

Billie had to suppress the urge to laugh out loud
at the comment. "Congratulations, Mr. Buford," she
said. "For turning over a new leaf." The smile she
gave him told him she wasn't falling for it for one
minute. "Now, if you'll excuse me, I'll leave you in
Dr. Barnaby's hands."

"Wait," he said. Billie paused at the door. "Look,
I was sort of hoping you could help me out with my
new lifestyle changes."

"Oh? Like in giving you the address of the nearest A.A. chapter?"

Cord grinned, then looked at Dr. Barnaby, who in turn looked aghast that Billie would say such a thing. "I think she likes me, Doc."

Dr. Barnaby grunted but didn't comment. It was obvious he didn't have a clue to what was going on between the two of them.

Cord slipped off the edge of the examining table and stepped closer to Billie. "I was hoping maybe you could put me on some kind of nutritional program," he said. "I figure if anyone knows how to take care of herself, it's you." The bold smile he offered told her how much he approved of her program.

The look she gave him told him she'd sooner step on broken glass.

"She can do that," Dr. Barnaby interrupted in an aim-to-please voice.

There was a tap at the door. Nurse Bradshaw peeked in. "Dr. Barnaby, Evelyn Simpson's here with her boy. He fell out of a tree. They think his arm is broken."

"Uh-oh." The old doctor started for the door.

"And Willie Holmes is on the phone, says he woke up with the hiccups and can't get rid of them for nothing."

Dr. Barnaby scratched his jaw. "Ask Willie if he can remember the last place he saw a frog run over by a car," he said, ignoring the look of disbelief that crossed Billie's face as he said it. "That'll cure him. And if he can't remember, tell him to mix some vinegar and sugar on a spoon and take it." He followed the nurse out, then glanced back at Cord. "Now, you take care not to get that wound infected, son. But if it does, I'll make you up a walnut poultice." He closed the door behind him.

Billie stood there for a moment, not knowing what to think or do. She met Cord's amused gaze.

"Sort of like waking up in the Twilight Zone, huh?" he said.

"Something like that," she said dully.

For the first time since she'd met him, Cord Buford turned serious. "Which is exactly why we need a new doctor in this town. Doc Barnaby means well, but each year I feel as if he's slipping further and further away."

Billie was surprised. "You're not insinuating that he has emotional problems, are you?"

"Naw, he's just getting senile." He paused. "His wife died a few years back. She did everything for him, made all his decisions. I don't think he ever bounced back from losing her."

Billie pondered it. "Thanks for telling me," she said. "It'll make it easier for me to deal with him."

"Does that mean we're on for lunch?"

She shook her head. "I thought we'd settled that."

"Okay, how about dinner?"

"No thank you."

"If you change your mind—"

"I won't." She dabbed his wound with an antiseptic.

Cord closed his hand around her wrist and held her fast. "You will. Sooner or later."

FOUR

The following evening Billie climbed the stairs to her apartment and found Cord sitting near the top. Leaning forward slightly, elbows on thighs, he looked very much at home. "What are you doing here?" she asked.

She was all business in a straight khaki skirt and white button-down Oxford blouse. Cord tried to imagine her in something flowing and transparent, and his gut tightened at the thought. She had wholesome good looks, but she was a little too reserved, a little too prim-and-proper. He wondered what she would look like naked, her body dewy and flushed from lovemaking. "I came to take you to dinner," he said in a tone that gave away none of his lewd thoughts.

"You don't take no for an answer, do you?" She said with a slight smile.

"You said no to dinner yesterday, you didn't say no to dinner today."

She started past him. He leaned to one side so she could get by, then tensed momentarily when he caught sight of her shapely legs.

He stood slowly and faced her, studying her quite openly. "How come you don't like me, Dr. Foster?"

She paused and fumbled in her purse for her keys. "I don't even know you, Mr. Buford."

"Call me Cord. I've never courted a doctor before," he said, noting the heightened color in her cheeks. He had caught the petite Dr. Foster off guard. Again.

"And you're not about to start with me." Billie unlocked the door with trembling fingers. Darn but the man had a way of unraveling her nerves. After a day spent bickering with Dr. Barnaby, she was not ready to face Cord Buford. "Now, if you'll excuse me—" She opened the door, stepped inside, and locked it. Cord reached up and tapped on the window as though to tell her something, but she merely pulled down the shade and left him standing there.

Five minutes later Billie stepped into the shower and tried to wash away all her frustrations of the day. She hummed the tune to an old Beatles' song. Dr. Barnaby had been his usual disagreeable self, second-guessing every one of her decisions. Billie washed her hair twice, soaped all over, and rinsed. She didn't know why she was going to the trouble.

In fifteen minutes she'd be sweating again. She *had* to do something about the broken air conditioner. She stepped out of the shower, dried, then pulled on her short bathrobe. She opened the bathroom door and headed for the kitchen. Her heart almost leapt from her chest when she saw Cord standing in her small living room looking as though he had every right to be there.

"How did you get in here?" she demanded, clutching her robe together at the top.

He held up her key ring. "You left these in the door."

She snatched the keys from him. "You had no right to come in uninvited."

"I knocked, but you were singing so loud in the shower, you must not have heard me."

Billie blushed so badly her ears burned. She often sang in the shower. It didn't matter that she couldn't hold a tune and that she probably sounded like a Guernsey cow giving birth. It relieved stress and put her in a better mood.

"Mind if I give you a piece of advice, Doc?" he said. When she didn't respond, he went on. "Keep your day job."

"Very funny. I believe you were just leaving?"

He ignored her. "Why is it so hot in here?" he asked, wiping sweat from his forehead.

"My air conditioner is broken. Don't try to change the subject."

"Where is it?"

"In the bedroom. Why?"

He stepped past her, going into her bedroom where he examined the small window unit. "Oh, man, this thing is bad," he said. He tried several buttons, then shook his head. "It's dead. Could I use your phone?"

"You come into my house uninvited, waltz into my bedroom like you own the place—why should you ask permission to use my phone?"

He grinned. "I don't blame you, I'd be bitchy, too, if I had to put up with Dr. Barnaby *and* this heat. Can't you open a window?"

"They've been painted shut."

He sat on the edge of her bed and reached for her telephone. "An old friend of mine works in an appliance store nearby. He might be able to fix you up with something right away."

Billie snatched her nightie and various under-things off the bed and stuffed them in a drawer. Why didn't he use the telephone in her kitchen, for heaven's sake? She wished she'd taken the time to make her bed that morning before going to the clinic. It unnerved her to have him sitting so casually on the sheets she slept on, resting his hand on the feather pillow that still bore the indentation of her head. He looked more rugged and virile than ever sitting there.

"Why are you so concerned about my air conditioner?" she asked as he punched a set of numbers on the phone.

" 'Cause I own this place," he said. "Nobody told me it needed a new air conditioner." He paused when someone answered on the other end of the line. "Let me speak to Pete, please. Yes, I'll hold."

Billie watched him wait to be connected to his party. He toyed with a pair of earrings she'd left on her night table, then, spying a small bottle of perfume, raised it to his nose. His gaze slid in her direction as though he recognized the scent.

"Stop snooping," she told him.

The smile became a grin. "I can't help it. You fascinate me."

"From what I hear, a woman only has to have a pulse to get your attention."

"Nurse Bradshaw has been talking about me again, hasn't she?" When Billie didn't answer, he persisted. "What did she say?"

"You're hazardous to a woman's heart."

"That's only because I haven't met the *right* woman. I believe there's a woman out there who can tame this wild heart of mine, Doc."

He was teasing her. Billie chuckled in spite of herself. "From what I hear, it would take a *big* woman. Maybe one who packs a shotgun as well."

He laughed, and the teasing light was back in his eyes. He wiped sweat from his brow. "It's hotter than a furnace in here, Doc. What does a guy have to do to get something cold to drink?"

When Cord came into the kitchen a few minutes later, Billie had prepared two glasses of iced tea. She handed him one. He drank it in one clean gulp, then set the glass down on the counter. "My friend's on his way. He's bringing two smaller units. One for the bedroom and one for the living room. I told him I'd hang around and help him carry them up."

She was openly relieved. "Thank you."

"You're welcome."

Billie gazed into his dark eyes for one breathless moment, startled by her own attraction to him. He projected an energy and power that her feminine side could not ignore. He might be the worst kind of scoundrel, but there was no denying that boyish charm that lay below the surface. The combination was a potent one. Add to that his good looks and a woman didn't stand a chance.

She realized suddenly that she was staring. And still in her bathrobe.

"Would you excuse me while I change?" she asked, wanting to put some distance between them and pull her thoughts together. She did not need to think of this man in any romantic light. "Help yourself to more tea," she added before she hurried out.

Cord watched her go, bathrobe billowing behind her in her rush to get away. She was as skittish as a treed kitten in a rainstorm. Was his reputation so bad that she feared being alone with him?

Nevertheless, one thing was for sure: She was interested. Deny it though she might, she found him attractive. Regardless of the fact that she didn't trust him and considered him the worst kind of womanizer.

He had to change her mind.

But how? She was much too smart to go out with him. How was he supposed to convince her he was a nice guy if she refused to spend time with him?

He was still pondering the thought when he drove home later, after having helped Pete install Billie's new air conditioners.

The quarter-mile driveway to the Buford estate was impressive, flanked by flowering azalea bushes, oleander, and tall live oaks. At one time Cord had looked forward to coming home at the end of the day. Now, he dreaded it, even more so when he saw the black stretch limo parked out front. That meant his father was home. Arthur Buford was in residence.

Cord could smell his father's pipe tobacco the minute he stepped through the front door, could hear him talking on the phone. His father never went anywhere without his pipe in one hand, a phone in the other. Cord walked past his father's study and started for the stairs.

"Cord, is that you?" Arthur Buford called out.

Cord turned on the stairs and descended with the enthusiasm of a prisoner entering solitary. He walked into his father's study and found him sitting behind a massive walnut desk holding a cordless phone to his ear. The older man hung up and faced his son squarely. "What the hell happened to your face?"

"I cut myself shaving."

"Looks like you were in another barroom brawl," Arthur said matter-of-factly. "I certainly hope she was worth it."

"You tell me. You've been keeping her up for the past six months."

"So you've taken to sleeping with my old girl-friends, eh? Come on, Cord, you can do better than that. I'm disappointed in you."

Cord merely shrugged.

His father sighed heavily. He looked old and tired, the lines around his mouth and eyes more pronounced. The past year had taken its toll. His hair was almost completely white. His skin sagged. "How long are you going to hold this grudge, Son? How long are you going to blame me for your mother's death? It's been a year now. Don't you think it's time to go on with our lives? We're never going to heal unless we let go of all this anger."

Cord stepped closer. "Save the speech. I don't believe a damn word of it. And I'm not going to let you forget what you did to my mother." He stalked out of the room, leaving his father slumped in his chair.

"How long have you had this cough, Mr. Helms?" Billie asked the man on the examining table as she pulled her stethoscope from her ears.

The man shrugged. "Couple of weeks. It keeps the wife up at night. Nothing seems to help. Sometimes I can't seem to catch my breath."

"Are you a smoker?"

"No, ma'am." He paused. "Probably just a summer virus," he said. "A couple of the weavers at work have it."

"You work at the textile mill?" she asked, her thoughts automatically turning to Cord.

He nodded. "In the weave room. Going on thirty years now."

"You wear some sort of mask over your mouth and nose for protection, don't you?" she asked. "To keep from breathing cotton dust?"

"We don't have a problem with cotton dust, so masks aren't required."

Billie made a note of it in his records. Surely, the health officials would know better than she if there were risks involved with employees breathing dust. "Well, it looks like a case of bronchitis. I'm going to write you a prescription for an inhaler, but what I really want you to do is take a few days off and rest. Do you have a vaporizer?" When he nodded, she went on, "Use it, please. And drink plenty of liquids."

"Thanks, Doc," he said as she handed him the prescriptions. He smiled. "Folks said you was pretty, but I had to see for myself. They was right."

Billie smiled at him as she followed him out of the room. "Stop flirting with me, or I'll give you an injection."

Nurse Bradshaw took the man's folder from Billie and led him toward the front office so he could pay. Billie took a minute to run to the tiny kitchen in back for a second cup of coffee. She had just taken her first sip when the nurse hurried in. "Is there any left?"

Billie nodded. "Enough for at least one more cup if you hurry."

While Naomi Bradshaw poured a cup, she studied Billie. "You're frowning. Is Doc giving you a hard time this morning?"

"No more than usual," Billie told her. She looked thoughtful. "Do you realize we've treated three bronchitis cases in less than a week?"

The nurse nodded. "Kind of early in the year for it, isn't it?"

"All three patients work at the mill."

"I'm not surprised. One gets sick, they all get sick. Just like the schools."

"So you don't think it could be work-related?"

"No," the nurse said emphatically. "I go inside

that mill every year to give flu shots, and I can tell you, it's clean as a whistle." She took a sip of her coffee. "Speaking of the mill, Cord Buford is in room two." She didn't sound pleased.

Billie spun around. "Why didn't you tell me?"

"I just did. He's here for his annual exam. Wants you to give it to him."

"I can't do his physical," Billie said, color creeping up her neck at the thought.

"Why not? You're a doctor, aren't you? Besides, Dr. B. just left. Homer Meed's prized filly is dropping a foal this morning, and they can't find the vet anywhere."

"Dr. Barnaby left to deliver a horse?" Billie said in disbelief.

"It happens," the nurse said. She eyed Billie steadily. "I hope you're not going to turn all calf-eyed over Cord Buford," she said. "I'd like to think you're too smart for that."

Billie squared her shoulders at the door to the exam room and marched in with all the briskness of an army doctor. "Good morning, Mr. Buford," she said, her heart skipping a beat at the sight of his broad, well-muscled chest. He sat on the table, a sheet wrapped around his middle. His flesh looked like buckskin against the white cotton fabric. "I see you're here for a physical. When was your last one?"

" 'Bout a year ago."

Billie reached inside his folder for the form that

she was to fill out. "Please get on the scale," she said. "I have to weigh and measure you."

He looked amused. "What are you going to measure?"

Her thoughts ran amuck. She silently berated herself. "Your height, of course."

"Of course. Should I keep the bed sheet or lose it?"

"Keep it!" Billie blushed when she realized she'd almost shouted the words. What in the world was wrong with her? She was a doctor, for heaven's sake. It wasn't as though she hadn't seen her share of male bodies.

"I was just asking," he said, slipping off the table and making his way toward the scales. Billie's gaze followed, taking in the wide back and shoulders, the taut hips that were well defined beneath the thin sheet. He stepped onto the scale. His calves were brown and slightly muscular and feathered with the same dark hair that covered his head and chest. "One-ninety-three," he said. "It never changes. Been that way since my senior year in college."

Billie stepped closer and peered over his shoulder. She caught the scent of clean male flesh. Her stomach fluttered. Being near him, his strong brown body, made her heart beat faster. "It says one-ninety-four."

He turned his head slightly, and their gazes locked. "That's 'cause I'm wearing this sheet. I could take it off, and you'd see—"

"That's fine, I believe you," she said, scribbling his weight onto his chart. She measured him. He was a quarter of an inch shy of six-and-a-half feet. "You can have a seat now," she said.

Over the next few minutes, Billie checked him carefully. Reflexes normal. His eyes, ears, nose, and throat were fine. Blood pressure excellent. Strong heartbeat. She palpated his abdomen and found no enlargements. "Does your family have a history of the following illnesses?" she asked, and read from her list.

Cord shook his head. "Is that it?" he asked, thinking it would be a good time to invite her to dinner. Which was the only reason he'd scheduled the physical to begin with.

Billie was about to answer when someone tapped on the door. Dr. Barnaby stuck his head in. "I'm back," he said. "I trust you didn't kill anyone while I was gone."

Billie was so happy to see the old doctor that she let the remark slide. "Great. Perhaps you wouldn't mind finishing up here for me." She stepped closer to the old doctor and whispered, "Mr. Buford needs a rectal exam and a prostate check." Dr. Barnaby nodded and took the form from her.

"Is there more?" Cord asked, straining to hear. He wanted the old doctor to leave so he could chat with Billie a moment in private.

"Only a couple of things," Billie said. She smiled

sweetly. Cord Buford would think twice the next time he sauntered into the clinic for a physical. "I'll leave you in Dr. Barnaby's hands now."

Cord watched the old doctor slip on a pair of rubber gloves. He swallowed. "Am I almost finished?"

"Not quite," Dr. Barnaby said. "Bend over."

FIVE

When Billie stepped out the back door of the clinic at the end of the day, she found Cord waiting for her. He clamped a fist around her wrist and pulled her to an abrupt halt. "That was a dirty rotten trick you pulled on me today."

Billie promptly disengaged her hand. "I beg your pardon?"

"You know what I'm talking about." He stepped closer, the dark scowl on his face telling her he was in no mood for games. "Sticking me with Barnaby the way you did. Why didn't you tell me what he was going to do?"

"And spoil the surprise?" Billie had to swallow the smile that threatened to erupt. "I trust everything came out okay?"

"Very funny, Dr. Foster."

She saw that he didn't look the least bit amused.

"Well, have a nice evening." She started for her apartment, and he stepped in front of her. "Okay, what do you want?" she demanded, her exasperation growing.

"Why didn't you do the exam yourself?"

"I thought it would be more comfortable if old buzzard lips did it," she said, using the nickname Nurse Bradshaw used when she was out of sorts with the old doctor.

"More comfortable for whom?" When she didn't answer right away, he went on. "Why didn't you tell me you had the hots for me?" he said, knowing the best way to get a reaction was to goad her.

"What?"

"You were afraid to do that exam because you're attracted to me, right? Because you didn't think you could remain professionally detached."

"You're crazy," she said, trying once more to go around him. Nevertheless, she knew he spoke the truth. It was the first time she could remember being ill at ease with a man's body. Except for the early days of her residency, of course. Somehow, it hadn't seemed right examining him, knowing how she felt.

"Why don't you admit it," he said. "You're attracted to me, or you wouldn't have rushed out of there as if the Devil himself was after you."

Billie sighed heavily. "Okay, so maybe I *do* find you attractive. Now would you kindly move out of my way?"

He looked surprised. "You really do? Then why are you giving me such a hard time about going out with me?"

"Just because I think you're attractive doesn't mean I'm stupid enough to date you," she said, then turned for her apartment.

He followed. "Why would that be stupid?"

She paused. "For one thing, I don't plan to be here forever, so a relationship is out of the question."

He chuckled. "I don't see why. Most of my . . . uh . . . relationships only last a few weeks anyway."

"So I've heard. Which brings us to the second reason I don't *want* to go out with you. I know your type. You're out for one thing. Guys like you were a dime a dozen in medical school." She stopped at the top of her stairs. "Why are you following me?"

"I thought you might want to invite me in."

"Why would I do that?"

"Why?" He thought about it. "Because you don't really know anybody else in this town. And because having me for a friend, as crummy as it sounds, is better than having no friends at all."

Billie considered it, knowing he had a point. When was the last time she'd had fun? School and work had left little time for it. And the truth of the matter was, she was tired of being alone. She missed the camaraderie of her fellow doctors in Virginia. She missed her family. Dr. Barnaby and Nurse Bradshaw weren't likely to include her in their circle of friends, and if they did, she couldn't imagine what they'd have in common. "What'd you have in mind?" she said at last.

The Seafood Shack sat on the edge of the river, a battered building that looked as though it might collapse under the next strong wind. Nevertheless, the parking lot was packed. Cord held open the front door and waited for Billie to pass through. He nodded and waved at several people as they waited to be seated. The spicy smells made Billie's mouth water.

"Do you like steamed shrimp and beer?" Cord asked when the waitress had seated them. Billie nodded, and he ordered a pound of shrimp to start off with. "There are nicer places in town," he said, "but none with better food."

Billie discovered he was right when she tasted the spiced shrimp and piping-hot hush puppies. "It's wonderful," she told him.

"See, isn't this better than sitting home all by yourself? Once you get out and meet folks, you might find you like it here."

"I guess I'm just homesick," Billie confessed while munching on a hush puppy. "I've always been so close to my family. My father isn't well.

I worry about him." She took a sip of her beer. "One of the reasons I wanted to be a doctor was so I could help my parents. They've worked hard all their lives. They made a lot of sacrifices for my education."

"And you're disappointed because you're not making the big bucks yet," he said. "So you can repay them for all they've done."

She nodded. "It'll be a few years before I can do the things I've always wanted to do for them. First I have to work off my loan here and clean up my other debts." She smiled suddenly. "I didn't mean to tell you my personal problems. See what half a beer does to me?"

He leaned back in his seat. "Has it ever occurred to you that your parents don't *expect* you to pay them back?" When Billie didn't respond right away, he went on. "Maybe they feel like you already have by successfully completing medical school. That's pretty impressive in itself."

"I still want to," she said matter-of-factly, then decided to change the subject. "How about you? What's your family like?"

"Just your average American family."

She chuckled. "I seriously doubt there's anything average about you *or* your family, Cord Buford."

"What do you mean?"

"Well, for one thing, you're rich. That hardly makes you typical of today's family."

"Well, don't hold it against me. My family had money long before I came along."

"And you're sleeping with your father's mistress—"

"I never said I was sleeping with her. We're old high school friends who had too much to drink that night and decided to go skinny-dipping just like when we were kids." He paused, and his voice was low when he continued. "She's in love with my father."

Billie couldn't imagine why a lovely young woman would want a man twice her age. Unless she was after his money. "Does your mother know about your father's affair?"

Cord's eyes clouded. "My mother is dead. She doesn't suspect a thing."

"I'm sorry," Billie said, noting the change that had come over him the minute she brought up his mother. "Do you have any brothers or sisters?"

"Nope. Just me."

She chuckled, hoping to take some of the tension out of the air. "I knew it. An only child. How awful for you. I'll bet you got everything you always wanted."

"Except for somebody to play with," he said. "I got tired of playing with my father's gold all by myself," he added, sarcasm slipping into his voice. "Could we talk about something else? This is a boring subject." He suddenly grinned. "I'd give up everything I had if you'd run away with me tomorrow."

She chuckled. "You're a slick talker, Cord Buford, but I'm not falling for it."

The waitress came up. "Ya'll want another beer?" she asked.

"Sure, why not?" Billie said. "I'm not on call tonight."

Cord smiled his approval. "Great. Just relax and have a good time."

"I'll relax," she said. "But under no circumstances will I go skinny-dipping with you later."

He grinned and saluted her with his empty beer mug. "Never say never, Dr. Foster."

They'd started on their second pound of shrimp and second beer when the band climbed onto the stage and started playing a slow country tune. "You want to dance?" Cord asked.

"I don't dance," she replied.

"What d'you mean, you don't dance?"

"I never learned how. When other girls my age were going to dances, I was studying at the public library. These days they'd refer to me as the class nerd."

"You're too pretty to be a nerd."

"My best friend worked at the public library. She'd sneak these big medical reference books out. I'd spend the whole weekend poring over them. *That* was my idea of a good time."

He chuckled. "I take back what I said. I think maybe you *were* a bit of a nerd. But don't worry. If you're nice, I'll personally teach you to dance."

Her pulse quickened at the thought of him holding her close on the dance floor. She took a sip of her beer. "What were you like growing up?" she asked, suddenly curious about the man sitting across from her.

He gave her a slip of a smile. "I didn't spend my weekends at the library."

She returned the smile. "Why am I not surprised?"

"I barely made it through high school," he confessed. "I flunked out of two colleges before my parents hit me with an ultimatum."

"Which was?"

"I pull my grades up or join the army. They were determined to see that I got an education one way or the other. The idea of going to boot camp was all the motivation I needed to get on track." He grinned. "I still got through college by the skin of my teeth. I think it helped that my father made large contributions every year." He paused. "I suppose that makes me sound like a spoiled little rich boy," he added. "Maybe I was. I like to think age has made me a bit more responsible." He paused. "Actually, when you think about it, *you* had the advantages."

She couldn't imagine what they were. "How do you figure?"

"You've always known what you wanted. You had something that mattered."

"And you didn't?"

"I work in the mills because it's expected of me, not because it gives my life great meaning. Which makes my father sad because he's looking forward to retirement, and I haven't indicated an interest in taking over."

"*Are* you interested in taking over?"

"I'm not sure. I used to think that's what I wanted. The mills have been in my family for years. It's the only thing I really know." He sighed and leaned back. "Honest to God, I don't know *what* I want. That's a depressing thought for a thirty-two-year-old man, isn't it?" He smiled, but it did not quite reach his eyes. "I've been sort of screwed up the past year, I think."

"Because of your mother's death?"

"Yeah, I guess so." He shifted in his seat as though suddenly uncomfortable. There had been times he hadn't even wanted to get out of bed in the morning. At least he was past that. "So, you want another beer?"

"No, this second one has already made me sleepy," she said, then yawned wide as if to prove her point. The band had suddenly grown too loud for conversation. "Would you mind very much if I asked you to take me home?"

"Not if you promise to invite me in for coffee.

You *do* drink coffee, don't you?" he asked quizzically, then motioned for the check.

"Gallons of it," she confessed. "I even took up smoking during my last year in medical school." When he looked surprised, she explained. "Even doctors get stressed out."

The waitress brought him the check, and he paid it. "Remind me to tell you about a good way to reduce stress," he said as he led her out.

She chose to ignore it.

They arrived back at Billie's apartment, and she put on a pot of coffee while Cord toyed with the knobs on her portable stereo. She stepped into the living room as a slow Johnny Mathis song began. Cord, having kicked his shoes off at the door, raised a finger and motioned for her to join him.

"What?"

"Come here, Doc. You're about to receive your first dance lesson."

She was instantly uneasy. "Uh, no, Cord. I'm not really—"

He pulled her into his arms before she could protest further. "Stop fussing and take my hand. Now put your arm around my waist."

Flustered and feeling a bit silly, she slipped her arm around his waist. "Like this?"

"Very good." He slipped his own hand around

her waist and let it rest at the small of her back. She felt tiny and fragile in his arms. He pulled her close so that their thighs were flush. He felt her stiffen. "You have to stand this close, Billie, or you won't be able to follow my lead."

His breath fanned her cheek as he spoke. It was the first time she'd heard him say her name, and she liked the way it sounded on his tongue. She was conscious of where he touched her; the firm grasp of his hand holding hers, his other resting low on her spine. He began to move to the music. His thigh brushed hers. Jolted by the contact, she stepped on his foot.

"Sorry."

"That's okay, just keep going and relax. You're too stiff."

"I can't help it."

"Close your eyes and don't think of anything but the music. Listen to the beat."

Billie tried to do as he said. She closed her eyes and listened to the music, but it was not easy to concentrate. Every nerve in her body stood at attention, and she was filled with a sense of expectancy.

The music stopped, and so did they. Billie raised her head, and their gazes locked and held for what seemed an eternity. She could feel her heart hammering in her throat, her pulse racing, blood coursing through her veins. Had someone come into the clinic with those symptoms, she would have ordered an EKG.

The look in his eyes said it all—he was going to kiss her. That knowledge filled her with anticipation.

Cord's grip tightened, her soft curves molded to the lean contours of his body. His look turned serious. A faint light flickered in the depths of his black eyes. "You're the first doctor I've ever kissed," he confessed.

"I've never kissed a rogue before," she said in a calm voice that belied her fluttering stomach and feeling of breathlessness.

"We're even then." The last word was smothered on her lips as his mouth captured hers in a kiss that completely shattered the fine thread of composure to which she clung. His kiss was hungry and urgent; his tongue eager and quick, darting past her teeth, exploring the moist lining of her mouth. It was devouring and soul-reaching; a kiss that fed and nurtured while it tantalized and delighted. Billie sank against his wide chest, succumbing to the domination of his mouth. Her emotions whirled out of control; her senses reeled as if short-circuited. It was like taking a wild carnival ride. All the while, his hands moved over her body restlessly, as though he couldn't get enough.

He explored the small of her back, then cupped her hips in his palms.

She caressed the length of his back, his wide shoulders.

He pulled her blouse from her skirt and sought her warm flesh.

She arched toward him. Her own greedy fingers explored the muscles in his shoulders and the corded tendons in his neck.

The need to inhale forced him to break the kiss, and they drank in deep gulps of air. A new song played on the radio.

Cord took a long, shuddering breath. "If I don't go now, I may never leave."

Her lips burned from the aftermath of his kiss, yet she ached for another. At the same time, she knew it was dangerous. She felt weak and confused and more vulnerable than ever. If he stayed another five minutes, they would end up in bed.

"Then you'd better go," she said, knowing it was the best decision if not the easiest.

He released her, despite wanting to stay, despite wanting to sweep her high in his arms and carry her into the bedroom. He had never desired a woman so much in his life. Even now, he was wondering when he'd see her again. He made his way to the door, then paused.

"How about dinner at my place Sunday?" he asked. "Lula's dyin' to meet you."

"Lula?"

"Our housekeeper. She runs the place."

"I'm on call Sunday."

"That's okay. We'll hang out by the pool in case the phone rings."

She wanted to go, but she didn't want to appear overly eager. She was certain Cord Buford had dated his share of eager women. "You say Lula will be there?" she asked, still hedging.

"She lives with us." He studied her expression. "You're not afraid to be alone with me, are you?"

"Of course not."

He grinned. "I'll pick you up at eleven."

SIX

Billie wanted to run the minute she spied the Buford estate. As Cord steered his car down the long driveway, the trees parted to reveal a magnificent Country French brick château that looked as though it had been snatched from the pages of *Southern Living*. "Oh, damn," she muttered, and shifted uncomfortably in her seat.

Cord reached for her hand and squeezed it. "Don't let it intimidate you, it's just a house."

"No, it's not just a house, it's a museum. How many rooms does this sucker have anyway?"

He chuckled, but it came out sounding dry and cynical. "Too many. Lula claims it's a bitch to clean."

"I wouldn't know," she muttered. "My own parents decided to build something more compact." She thought of the tiny house she'd grown up in that never had enough closets or bathrooms.

Cord laughed. "I *do* believe our new doctor is

a bit of a snob," he said, regarding her with those humorous black eyes.

"How do you figure?" she said, thinking of all the categories he could place her in, that had to be the one she least fit into.

"You don't think a person's up-to-snuff unless they've struggled or despaired most of their lives. Money isn't the answer to everything, Billie. Rich people have problems. They get old; they suffer and die."

"Yes, but they do it in those classy retirement villages with a nurse beside them," she said. "Don't try to convince me people are created equal, Cord. That's a crock. That's something rich people tell themselves so they won't feel guilty over the homeless situation or starving children in Africa. The rich go right on buying their mink coats—"

"My mother was an animal-rights activist," he interrupted. "She wore only fake stuff."

Billie regarded him with an amused look. "Well, I guess that's one thing she and I would've had in common. I wear the fake stuff too."

"She owned very little jewelry," he added. "And most of the time she was dressed in worn jeans and a sweatshirt. She drove an old yellow pickup truck that was forever breaking down on her. She ran an adoption program for pets, you see. Said it was crazy to wear nice clothes when you were always holding a cat or dog in your arms."

"Your mother sounds like someone I would have enjoyed knowing." That look came back into his eyes. "How'd she die?"

Cord glanced out his side window. "An accident. She was speeding and hit a tree." He finally looked at her. "Want to know *why* she was speeding?" He didn't wait for her to answer. "She was leaving my father. It had taken her years to work up the nerve. She didn't leave in the beginning because of me. Then my grandmother suffered a stroke shortly after I started college, and my mother moved her in with us and spent the next eight or nine years looking after her. Once my grandmother died and I was grown, there was no reason for her to stay." He offered her a mirthless smile. "I reckon once she had the opportunity to finally get out, she couldn't do it fast enough."

"I'm sorry, Cord." Billie knew what it was like to lose someone close. Even though the pain lessened as time went on, one never recovered from the loss.

He smiled, leaned over, and kissed the tip of her nose. "You ready to go in?" he asked. "Or would you rather Lula bring us a tray out to the car?"

"I'm ready."

The stout housekeeper studied Billie with a critical eye, then nodded her gray head in approval. "I *do* declare, she's the prettiest little thing I ever did see. Next to your mama, of course."

Cord turned to Billie. "That's quite a compliment coming from Lula," he said. "Nobody has ever come *close* to comparing with my mother."

"A little skinny," the woman added, taking a closer look at Billie's slight build. "But we can do something about that."

"It's nice to meet you, Lula," Billie said, thinking the woman had the warmest brown eyes she'd ever seen. Instinct told her it was Lula who'd pulled Cord through the loss of his mother.

"Where are your manners, Cordell Buford?" Lula said, popping him on the shoulder with a serving spoon. "Take the good doctor out on the patio and pour her some of that lemonade I made."

"Yes, ma'am," Cord said, grabbing Billie's hand and pulling her toward the back door. "Hurry before she gets out her rolling pin," he added with a chuckle.

The patio was a terrace of sorts, decorated with navy canvas chairs and chaise longues and shaded with large navy-and-white striped awnings. It overlooked a sparkling, kidney-shaped pool. Cord poured them each a glass of lemonade. "You can change into your bathing suit over there," he said, motioning to a wing of the house he claimed were guest quarters.

Billie drank half of her lemonade before going into the guest area to change. She noted a suite of rooms decorated in a soothing mint-green color with white overstuffed sofas and chairs, and she wondered if Cord's mother had decorated it. Like the kitchen, it was warm and tasteful, a contrast to the rather austere decor in the living room. Billie changed in one of the bedrooms. Her bathing suit, like everything else she owned, was old and worn. But the look in Cord's eyes when she stepped outside with a towel draped over her shoulders told her she didn't look too shabby nonetheless.

"Nice," he said. "You doctors really know how to take care of yourselves."

Billie smiled to hide her discomfort over his thorough perusal. "See what clean living does for you?" she said. At the same time she couldn't help but notice how good he looked in his own suit. He'd stripped off his shirt. There wasn't an ounce of fat on the man's entire body. Only dark brown skin and black chest hair. Knowing his reputation, she decided clean living had nothing to do with the way a person looked. It had to be in the genes. She was still staring when he dived into the pool.

Cord surfaced and shook his head, throwing tiny droplets everywhere. "Aren't you coming in?"

Billie dropped her towel at the side of the pool. "Yes, but I don't want to get my hair wet. In case my answering service calls." She had given her service Cord's telephone number in case of an emergency.

Cord grinned, placed his palms flat on the side of the pool, and propelled his lean body out. His stance was powerful. "You shouldn't have told me that, Dr. Foster."

Billie noted the almost feral look on his face. She took a step back. "What do you mean?"

All at once he sprang forward, grabbed one of her hands, and literally threw her over his shoulder. Billie screamed. "What are you doing? Put me down, you big oaf!"

"No way, lady. You're about to pay for that little trick you pulled on me at the clinic the other day."

Billie knew she was about to be good and doused. "No, wait, Cord," she cried, pounding on his back. "That wasn't a trick. That was all part of your exam."

"Well, next time be sure and tell Dr. Barnaby not to stick his hands in a freezer before he decides to check me out *down there.*" Cord took off in a run and jumped into the pool, creating enough of a splash for three men his size.

Billie opened her mouth to protest, and her mouth instantly filled with water. She kicked herself free of Cord and started to swim away, but he grabbed one ankle and pulled her back. She came up coughing and sputtering for all she was worth. "You big bully!" she cried. "Let me go!"

"Say 'uncle,'" he demanded, wearing that cocky

grin she'd come to know so well in such a short time.

"Never!"

He dunked her. She bobbed up, took a swipe at him, and missed.

"Say 'Cord is the best-looking thing I've ever laid eyes on,' " he taunted, cupping the top of her head with his palm. It was plain as the look on his face what he intended to do.

"You dunk me again, and I swear you're going to regret the day you met me, Cord Buford," she said. All at once he let her go, and the smile faded with an abruptness that was startling. He looked past her. She swung around and found an older man standing near the pool. He was handsome despite his age. His silver-white hair and neat charcoal suit made him look like a tycoon out of *Money* magazine. The man smiled, and Billie noted his resemblance to Cord immediately.

"You didn't tell me you were having company today, Son," he said.

Cord's jaw was hard; all the light had disappeared from his eyes. "I thought you were going out of town."

"My plans changed." The man turned to Billie. "Aren't you going to introduce me to your friend?"

Cord glanced at Billie. "This is Dr. Billie Foster," he said. "Billie, meet my father, Arthur Buford."

Billie reached up to shake the man's outstretched

hand, apologizing for the fact that she was wet. "Nice to meet you, Mr. Buford," she replied, wishing she understood the sudden coldness in Cord's voice.

If the man noticed his son's lack of enthusiasm in seeing him, he didn't say anything. "So you're the new doctor I've been hearing about. Welcome to Ruckers. I understand you made quite an impression with some of our employees at the mill. They claim you're much better-looking than Doc Barnaby." He smiled again. "Well, I'll leave you two now. I'm glad you could pay us a visit, Dr. Foster. Please come again."

Billie returned his smile. Although he was nice enough, he was a little too formal, a little too reserved. "Call me Billie."

The man nodded, then offered a brief nod to his son. "See you around, Cord."

Cord didn't speak until they were alone. "What was that all about?" he asked. "You didn't tell me you were treating some of our mill workers."

Billie pulled herself out of the pool, and he followed. "Several of them have come in with bronchitis." She reached for her towel and mopped her face and hair.

"Why didn't you tell me?"

She regarded him with a curious look. "Why should I? I didn't feel the cases were work-related at the time, and I don't make a habit of discussing my patients with other people."

He reached for his own towel. "Wait a minute, you lost me. What do you mean, you didn't think the cases were work-related at the time? Does that mean you've changed your mind?"

She shrugged. "I'm not sure. I can understand co-workers passing a cold around, but I can't figure how several of your weavers have bronchitis." She paused. "Unless they're breathing something that—"

"I hope you're not insinuating what I think you are," he said, studying her carefully. "Our mills are in compliance with all government regulations, and our employees follow the safety guidelines to a *T*."

"How can you be so sure?"

"Because I personally see to it." He dried himself and slung the towel around his neck. "A few years back there was an accident at a mill north of Atlanta. A couple of people died. Thank God it wasn't one of ours. But it got me to thinking. Some of our equipment was old; some of our employees weren't properly trained. So I created a task force and within six months had all of our mills operating at the safest possible level. I like to think we're setting standards for other mills. You'd be surprised how many of them contact us for advice."

"Well, that certainly puts my mind at ease," Billie said, taking a seat in one of the chairs. "Your plant manager told me pretty much the same thing."

He arched one brow. "You contacted Bill Crenshaw?"

"I called him a couple of days ago. Why, did I do the wrong thing?"

"Of course not. Bill's like one of the family. I just don't understand why you didn't come to me."

"I was merely going through the proper channels," she said. "Besides, I didn't know how involved you were with the mill."

Once again his eyes clouded. "I used to be more involved than I am now."

"It has something to do with your father, doesn't it?"

He looked surprised. "How'd you know?"

"I thought the pool would freeze over with those icy looks you were giving him."

"We don't get along, haven't got along for a long time now."

"Since your mother died?"

"You ask a lot of questions, Doc." He paused. "But, yeah, my mother's death has a lot to do with it. That and the fact that he's a selfish bastard and always has been. My mother was miserable married to him, but he refused to give her a divorce. Which is why she up and left the way she did. I hold him personally responsible for her death."

"Have you told your father how you feel?"

"He knows."

Billie was about to respond when Lula opened the back door. "Your answering service is on the phone, Dr. Foster."

Billie looked at Cord. "I knew it was too good to be true." She rose from her seat and hurried inside. When Cord walked into the kitchen a moment later, she was just hanging up.

"What is it?" he asked.

She sighed. "Somebody named Gus thinks he broke his ankle falling out of his pickup truck this morning."

Cord nodded. "That'd be Gus Jennings. I'll bet he was drunk when he did it."

"Well, I told him to meet me at the clinic so I could X-ray it. I'm sorry, but I have to go."

"I'll drive you."

"I should have brought my car."

"Gus is a mean drunk, Billie. I'd rather you not deal with him alone. I'm sure Lula can keep dinner warm."

Lula nodded from the other side of the kitchen. "It won't be ready for another hour anyway. I'll turn the oven down."

"Are you sure?" Billie asked. "I hate to interfere with your plans."

Lula dried her hands on a dish towel. "Go with her, Cord," she said. "I know what a nasty temper old Gus has." She regarded Billie. "He wrecked his truck last year, and Shorty had to pick him up in the ambulance. Well, Shorty said something Gus didn't like, and Gus punched him in the face."

"It's settled," Cord told Billie. "I'm going."

They were on their way in a matter of minutes. While Cord drove, Billie tried to repair her face and hair in the mirror attached to the sun visor. Cord grinned when she caught him staring. "Don't mind me," he said. "I like watching you do that."

"Do what?"

"Primp."

"I'm not primping. I can't very well walk into the clinic with my hair all over the place."

"Don't lie, Dr. Foster, I know primping when I see it."

She closed the mirror and moved the visor. "And I suppose that overinflated ego of yours tells you I'm doing it for your benefit."

"You got it. But you'd sooner hold a live snake than admit it."

Gus Jennings was a wiry old man with a snarled gray beard and bushy brows. He was carried into the clinic, spewing four-letter words, by an overweight wife and a man he claimed was his son-in-law. Cord immediately stepped in. "You shouldn't be lifting him, Bea," he told the grunting woman as he took over.

"Just put him there," Billie said, motioning to the table next to the X-ray machine.

"Who the hell are you?" the old man demanded.

Billie regarded him. "I'm Dr. Foster. How did you hurt your ankle?"

"Fell outta my damn truck this morning. Been hurtin' like the devil ever since."

"Can you walk on it?"

The man glared at her. "If'n I could walk on it, I would'na had my family carry me in like I was a side of beef, now would I?"

Cord put a hand on the old man's shoulder. "Now, now, Gus, there's no reason to yell at Doc Foster. She has to ask these things in order to make a diagnosis."

Gus gave a snort of disgust, then glanced at his wife, who was standing in the doorway. "D'you bring my tonic in from the truck?" The woman nodded, pulled a flask from her full skirt, and handed it to him.

"What is that?" Billie asked when he opened it and she caught the offensive smell.

"Something to fight off arthritis."

"I didn't know you had arthritis," Cord said.

Gus took a swig, then wiped his mouth with the back of his hand. "Don't. Stuff must work, huh?"

Billie saw Cord smile. "Well, you'll have to put that away for me to examine you," she said. She looked toward his wife and son-in-law. "I'm going to have to ask you two to wait out front," she told them. "I need to get an X ray." They hesitated. "It won't take long," she assured them.

Gus let fly a few more colorful expletives as Billie and Cord had to adjust his ankle several times in order to get a clear picture. By the time Billie had finished X-raying the man, her nerves were badly frazzled. "It's fractured," she announced some minutes later after she'd read the X ray. "I'm going to have to send you to the hospital, Mr. Jennings."

"The hospital!" he bellowed so loudly, they both jumped. "You mean clear to the next town?"

"That's right. You need a cast."

He pounded his fist on the examining table. "Aw, sh—!"

"That's no way to talk to Doc Foster, Gus," Cord reminded him. "She's only trying to help. Maybe next time you'll be more careful getting out of your truck."

"Why don't you mind your own damn business, Cord Buford?" the old man said. "What are you doing here anyhow? You ain't no doctor."

"I'm assisting the doctor today."

Gus looked from one to the other. "What s'matter, cain't she get out of her britches by herself?"

Billie's face flamed. Cord's jaw became rigid. He grabbed Gus by the collar. Billie put her hand on his arm. "Don't," she said. She saw him hesitate, then relax his grip. He released the man. Billie gave a sigh of relief. "I can certainly understand Mr. Jennings's reluctance to drive all the way to the next town for treatment when we're perfectly capable of setting his ankle ourselves," she said. Gus gave Cord a smug look as he straightened his collar.

Cord offered her a baffled look. "We are?"

"Of course. You remember how we treated the last broken ankle," she told him, arching one brow high on her head as though daring him to contradict her.

Cord caught on fast. "Oh, yeah, I remember." Suddenly, he frowned. "But, Doc, that patient died."

Billie shrugged, noting they had Gus's undivided attention. "Well, that wasn't our fault, Cord. How were we supposed to know his cataclysmic artery was going to burst inside his flotsam flibbertigibbet?"

"That's true," Cord said, as though it made perfect sense.

"What the hell's a fibergibit?" Gus said.

"Flibbertigibbet," Billie corrected, spelling it slowly for him.

"It's a vessel running from the ankle to the heart," Cord told him.

"And this patient's flibbertigibbet burst when Cord had to rebreak his ankle."

"Rebreak it?" Gus almost cried. "What the hell for?"

"It's standard procedure, Mr. Jennings," Billie said, scribbling something on his chart. "We can't set a fracture that occurred hours ago." She pointed to his bony ankle. "See how crooked it is? We'll have to rebreak it and straighten it before we can put it in a cast."

"Oh, no, Doc, it's always been this crooked," Gus

said hurriedly. "Just look at my other'n." He slid his other leg up so Billie could get a good look at the ankle. It was just as crooked, just as bony.

"Oh, no," she said, sharing a sad look with Cord.

Cord shook his head. "You're not thinking what I think you're thinking?"

"What's she thinking?" Gus asked, looking from one to the other.

"That we might have to break both ankles."

"What!" Gus threw a protective hand over each ankle.

"You know where to find my surgical hammer, don't you, Cord?" Billie asked, washing her hands at the sink and slipping on a pair of rubber gloves.

"Wait!" Gus cried. "Wait just a damn minute." He continued to cover his ankles. "You two are crazy, you know that? Crazy as hell if you think I'm gonna let you break both my ankles. Call my family back in here. I don't care if we have to drive all the way to Texas for a good doctor. I ain't lettin' neither one of you touch me."

Billie's face was a mask of disappointment. "But, Mr. Jennings—" She clasped her hands together in front of her. "I know I can do it," she said, her expression hopeful. "If you'll only give me a chance."

"You ought to let her have a swing at it, Gus," Cord told him. "It'd sure make her happy after what happened last time."

"Don't touch me!" Gus said, when Billie stepped

closer. He reached into his pocket. "I've got a pocketknife. I'll use it on the first one who comes near me." He called out for his wife and son-in-law, and they came running. They paused in the doorway. "Get me to the hospital!" Gus demanded. "Afore these people kill me." Without a word the two lifted him off the table and made for the doorway, bumping Gus's fractured ankle twice before they made it through the opening. He was still cussing as they rushed him out the front door.

Billie met Cord's gaze, and they burst into laughter.

"By the way," he said, as they locked up. "What the heck is a flibbertigibbet?"

She chuckled. "I think it's a scatterbrained person. I was asked to spell it during our high school spelling bee. I couldn't, and I lost my chance to go to the national." She grinned. "I've since learned to spell it."

SEVEN

True to her word, Lula kept dinner hot until they returned. Billie and Cord dined on a stuffed crown roast, fettuccine noodles, and fresh asparagus. Lula had made a fudge pecan pie for dessert and insisted Billie have a small slice even though she claimed she couldn't hold another bite. Once Billie declared it the best meal she'd ever tasted, Cord carried two cups of coffee out back so they could drink it on a stuffed settee next to the pool.

It was a clear, star-filled night. They sipped their coffee in companionable silence and listened to the crickets. Billie was aware of Cord's thigh touching hers, the smell of his after-shave. "I love the sky at night," she said, leaning back against the settee, trying to relax now that they were alone. The camaraderie they'd experienced earlier was still with them, but added to it was an awareness that made them both a bit tense. Her whole being seemed to be filled with a sense of waiting. "My brother and I received a telescope one Christmas," she went on. "We used to stare through it for hours, until our mother called us in for bed. He taught me the names of all the constellations. I've forgotten most of them, though," she added.

"Where is he now?"

Billie didn't answer for a minute. "He died before I started high school. Leukemia." She saw the startled look Cord gave her, and she smiled gently. "It came as no surprise. He'd had it for a couple of years." She sighed. "I think I probably read every book on the illness I could find during the time he was sick. I kept hoping to discover something about the disease that everybody else had overlooked. Something that would save his life. Even before I decided to become a doctor, I fantasized about finding a cure for leukemia."

"So now I know why you decided to become a doctor," Cord said. "But why a general practitioner? Why not a cancer specialist?"

"I couldn't do it, Cord," she said. "I didn't have it in me. I watched my brother die. It was as if our whole family had cancer by the time it was over." She paused and sighed. "As I said, I just didn't have it in me. It was too close to my heart, I suppose."

"Are you happy with what you're doing?"

She nodded. "I enjoy being a general practitioner,

the old-fashioned kind of doctor. I enjoy treating a variety of symptoms. It sort of keeps me on my toes, so to speak." She grew serious. "I know I'm going to run into cancer patients from time to time, and I'm prepared for that. I simply don't want it to be my main focus. The way it was when my brother was ill." She chuckled softly after a moment. "Of course, that was before I came to Ruckers. Now, my main focus is how to get through another day with Dr. Barnaby."

Cord laughed as well. "I'd think after dealing with Gus Jennings, Dr. Barnaby would be a piece of cake."

She gave a snort. "I don't know why Gus's wife puts up with him."

"Maybe she loves him."

"I can't imagine why."

Cord studied her in the moonlight. "You ever been in love, Doc?"

She glanced at him, then back at the sky. "I thought I was once."

"What happened?"

"He was forced to drop out of medical school and get a full-time job. Which was a shame because he would have made a wonderful doctor. We lost touch." She paused, and when she spoke again, there was a bitter ring to her voice. "You could tell which students were struggling to pay for medical school," she said. "They were the ones who worked hardest in class. Those who could easily afford it didn't seem to take it as seriously as the rest of us."

"Another reason for you to hate wealthy people," Cord said, giving her a small smile.

"I don't hate wealthy people," she said, then paused when she saw his knowing look. "Okay, maybe I resent them just a little. I feel if my parents had had money, maybe they could have kept my brother alive a little longer. Maybe they could have sent him to a better hospital."

"Money didn't keep my mother alive," Cord told her.

The realization jolted her, and she was forced to reexamine the small prejudices she'd tucked away inside her heart so many years before as she'd pondered the reasons for her brother's death. At fifteen, she'd needed something or someone to blame it on. "Yes, well, that's true," she said, the admission dredged up from a place of logic and reason. In the emergency room she'd pulled sheets over the faces of rich and poor alike. Finally, having settled that thought in her mind, she turned and found him watching her, an intense look on his face.

"What?"

"You're beautiful." He chuckled softly and slipped his arm around her when she looked suddenly uneasy. "Why does it make you uncomfortable for me to tell you that?"

"I don't feel beautiful."

"Then you obviously haven't looked in a mirror lately." He gazed at her, his face close, his onyx eyes gentle and contemplative. "Has there been anyone else in your life since your medical student?" he asked.

"There hasn't been time."

"What about now?" He leaned closer.

"You know I'm only here temporarily."

"So you've told me at least a dozen times," he said. "Don't you plan to have some sort of life outside the clinic while you're here?" When she didn't answer right away, he went on. "You know what I think?"

"What?"

"I think you'd like to get involved with me, but you're afraid."

"Of what?"

"That we'll fall in love and you'll end up staying in this place."

Billie almost laughed out loud. She couldn't imagine a man like Cord falling in love with anyone for very long. As soon as the newness wore off, he'd lose interest. "You're kidding, right?"

"Be honest, Doc, the thought *has* crossed your mind. It's crossed mine, and you know what? It scares me to death."

"What could you possibly be afraid of?" she asked, barely able to breathe because of his nearness.

"Of falling in love with you, what else? I've never really been seriously in love, other than those brief periods of infatuation I went through in college. Why wouldn't I be scared?"

Billie gazed back at him, too stunned to speak. Finally, she found her voice. "It's getting late, Cord."

"You don't believe me. You think this is just a ploy to get you in the sack. You don't think I have any scruples whatsoever, do you?"

"Scruples? Is that what you call sleeping with your father's mistress?"

"We've already been through all that. Sheila and I partied together a few times. So what?" He couldn't understand why she didn't believe him. Not only that, he couldn't figure why a woman like Billie, who had everything going for her, would be jealous of a woman like Sheila, whose only ambition in life was to marry a rich man. Still, he liked to think that maybe, *just maybe*, Billie was jealous of any woman he spent time with. Maybe now wasn't the time to declare himself innocent of knowing Sheila in the biblical sense. "Does my . . . er . . . friendship with Sheila bother you?" he asked hopefully.

"As a physician, I can't condone sleeping around."

He studied her in the darkness. Now what the hell kind of answer was that? It gave him nothing to go on. He didn't want her opinion as a professional; he wanted her to answer as a woman. "You know what your problem is, Billie Foster?" he said. "You've been reading too many medical books."

"What's that supposed to mean?"

"Maybe you've lost touch with what the human body is really about. It's not just a collection of muscle, bone, and tissue, you know. It's feeling and emotion as well." He stroked her arm as he talked, and Billie shivered involuntarily. "It's sensation. Or has it been so long since you've been with a man that you've forgotten?"

Billie shifted uneasily on her seat. It was too easy to get lost in the low, husky sound of his voice. She felt a delicious swooping pull low in her stomach. "Our bodies also come equipped with a conscience," she said, trying to make her voice sound as reasonable and matter-of-fact as she could manage. "To remind us that we don't simply do something because it feels good at the moment. It also reminds us of the risks involved." Why was she telling him this? Awkwardly, she looked away.

"I'm a big boy, Billie. I know the risks, and I take precautions." The huskiness lingered in his tone.

Uncertainty made her respond more harshly than she'd meant to. "It's none of my business."

"I think maybe this is your way of *making* it your business."

She snapped her head up, too startled by his suggestion to object. A hot blush crept up her neck. She started to get up, and he laughed and pulled her down onto his lap. Automatically, she tried to resist, but he merely gripped her more tightly. She felt suddenly ill-equipped to deal with her situation.

"You know, the sooner you stop fighting this thing between us, the sooner we're going to be able to do something about it."

Billie opened her mouth to protest, then closed it. The silence stretched between them, taut with tension that had been building all afternoon. His steady gaze impaled her, her stomach churned with anxiety, and she felt as if all the air had been sucked from her lungs. She felt like a volcano ready to erupt, and it was all his fault. Why did he have to be so damnably handsome, so irresistibly masculine? She noted the square jaw, shadowed with his beard; the mouth, firm and sensual and curled slightly at the corners as though on the verge of smiling. She wanted to believe she was drawn to him because of loneliness and because she missed her family, but she knew better. She couldn't get him out of her mind no matter how she tried. She *did* wonder about his sex life and if he was finding comfort in the arms of his father's mistress. The thought never failed to tear at her insides. She didn't want him to be with another woman. Not when she wanted him so desperately for herself. She liked Cord Buford more than she wanted to admit. Heck, she could even be falling in love with him, for all she knew. "What do you suggest?" she asked as waves of apprehension swept through her, as thrilling as they were frightening.

He held her snugly. When he spoke, his breath was hot against her cheek. "Let me take you home, and I'll show you."

Cord drove her home in silence. Halfway there, he reached for her hand, raised it to his lips, and kissed it, then placed it on his thigh and covered it with his own. The gesture was intimate and possessive and sent a shimmer of warmth through Billie. His muscles were hard beneath her fingertips, making her acutely aware of the power and strength so inherent in him. By the time he pulled in the driveway behind the clinic, her stomach was tied in knots.

Cord cut the engine and studied her in the semidarkness, his expression quizzical. "You okay?"

She smiled and nodded, despite struggling with her own uncertainties. She had thought of herself as simply a doctor for so long, she had forgotten all about being a woman. Where had all these insecurities come from, this sense of inadequacy? "I'm fine," she said, giving him what she hoped was her most convincing smile. It must've worked. He climbed out, then helped her out a moment later. Wordlessly, he followed her up the stairs, took her key, and unlocked the door. He pushed it open and motioned for her to pass through first.

"You haven't spoken two words since we left my place," he said as he handed her the key.

Billie stuffed the keys in her purse before setting it on the table. She kicked off her shoes, but her movements were awkward and stilted. She felt self-conscious, knowing he watched her every move. "I'm nervous."

He noted the lines of tension around her mouth, and he wished there was something he could do to make her relax. Why did she have to be anxious when his own heart was literally leaping for joy at the thought of being with her? At the same time he didn't want to rush her. He wanted their first time together to be something she would remember for a long time. Suddenly, he felt unsure. Why did it have to matter so much? She had agreed to this despite the fact she was only there temporarily. Why should he care what happened afterward? But he *did* care, dammit. For once in his life he *wasn't* just looking for a roll in the hay. He wanted to feel something *after* it was all over.

"I don't have to stay," he said at last, then wondered where it had come from. Certainly not from the Cordell Buford he'd come to know and love.

Billie gazed back at him with a strange surge of affection. He was willing to back off if she needed him to. That knowledge touched her deep inside where she had felt empty for so long, an emptiness that could not be filled despite a loving family and busy career. Instead of saying anything, she walked over to him, feeling smaller than ever in her stocking feet. She placed her hand against his chest and felt the muscles tighten in response. He was feeling as vulnerable as she was. "I want you to stay," she whispered softly.

Relief showed in his face by the subtle relaxing of his jaw. He smiled, and the warmth echoed in his voice and lit up his eyes. He wondered if she knew he'd been holding his breath. "I think I can fit it into my schedule." Her own smile was faint and tentative as she slid her hand down the length of his arm and captured his fingers, entwining them with hers. She led him from the room into the short hallway. He wondered if she had any idea how utterly charming the simple gesture was, how sweet. At that moment he would have let her lead him across a bed of hot coals.

They ended up in her bedroom. Billie released him and made her way to the night table and switched on a lamp. From the doorway Cord glanced around the room. It looked much the same as before, only this time the bed was neatly made. Her bathrobe was draped over a chair, and a pair of sneakers, no bigger than a child's, sat on the floor in front of the dresser. He was reminded once again how small she was. How delicate. He closed the door and made his way toward her, his eyes never leaving her face.

Billie stood there breathlessly, waiting for him

to touch her, the moment made sweeter because he took his time. Her stomach fluttered wildly, feeling as though it would catapult into her rib cage if he didn't pull her into his arms soon. Instead, he stopped within an inch of touching her. She moaned inwardly. He raised a big hand to her face and cupped her cheek. The simple act was both gentle and tender, a direct contradiction to the power and strength she suspected he was capable of. A hot ache grew in her throat and spread to her chest. When she tried to speak, her voice wavered.

"I only have one request."

"Name it."

"You don't sleep around if you're going to sleep with me," she said as casually as she could manage.

Amusement flickered in his dark eyes and nudged the corners of his mouth. "You underestimate yourself, Doc. What makes you think I'd want to?"

A new and unexpected warmth surged through her. She stared wordlessly, her heart pounding in her chest like Congo drums. He closed the brief distance between them, clasped her body tightly to his, and held her for a long, silent moment. He felt lean and hard against her own softness. Billie relaxed, sinking into his embrace. He gazed down at her through olive-black eyes only an instant before dipping his head and capturing her lips.

The kiss was slow and thoughtful, surprisingly gentle. Nevertheless, it sent her thoughts into a wild spin. As his tongue teased the seam of her lips, Billie parted them and raised on tiptoe, wrapping her arms around his neck tightly, as though half-afraid he might pull away.

Cord moaned against her open mouth as he felt her body strain toward him. Until that moment he'd prided himself on his control. It vanished, along with his promise to himself to take it slow. Crushing her to him, he took her mouth with a savage intensity that surprised him as much as it did her. His tongue became forceful and thrusting as if its one thought was to devour. Billie clung to him, weak, confused, and shivery, her mouth on fire. She was reminded of the intense heat that welded metal together. Equally hot were his hands as he reached around and cupped her behind. There was the sound of cotton rubbing against nylon as he slid her skirt upward. A moment later he'd wedged those same hands inside her pantyhose, kneading her soft hips before moving around to the front.

Billie's ears roared as eager fingers sought and found her moist heat. She arched against his open palm as he teased and tormented the area between her thighs until she feared her body would short-circuit and explode. Without breaking the kiss, he walked her backward until she felt the mattress against the back of her thighs. Very gently, he eased her down onto the bed, following as she went. With deft but impatient fingers he removed her clothes; skirt and blouse were tossed aside to fall on the floor with a whisper. Her slip, pantyhose, and panties followed. Finally, Billie was naked. His eyes raked boldly over her as though photographing in mind each detail.

"I was right," he said, his voice a thick whisper. "You *are* beautiful." Reclaiming her lips, he pulled her into his arms, almost roughly. Finally, he broke the kiss so he could sample the rest of her. He kissed the valley between her breasts before taking each pink nipple into his mouth. He sucked and teased them with his teeth until they were twin quivering peaks. Billie reached for him, but he escaped her eager hands and slid farther down her body, tonguing her navel, nipping her belly playfully with his teeth.

She felt his breath before she felt his mouth; warm, moist air fanning her thighs and the dark brown triangle that covered her femininity. She froze, anticipating his next move. Soft as a whisper, he kissed her.

"Cord." His name rolled off her lips like warm honey.

He cupped her buttocks, lifted her slightly, and tasted all that she had to offer. Billie sucked her breath in sharply as his mouth and tongue made intimate contact with the warm, musky areas of her body. His tongue moved upward, seeking the small bud that housed her desire. He teased her, flicking his tongue soft as a butterfly's wing. Billie cried out softly, his name a whimper on her lips. She tensed as passion radiated from the soft core of her body, building gradually until it flamed white-hot and hurtled her beyond the point of return. Until she was numb and her thoughts as fragmented as the love words he spoke to her.

Cord tore himself away only long enough to undress, leaving his clothes puddled beside hers. Billie gazed at him through passion-hazed eyes, reacquainting herself with his magnificent body as she watched him take the necessary precautions. Her affections deepened. The mattress dipped as he joined her once again, this time parting her legs. She welcomed him into her body, sheathing him so tightly, he swore under his breath. She clung to him, meeting each thrust, discovering his tempo as she had the night they'd danced in her living room. He buried his face against her neck and shuddered in her arms, only a second after her own climax.

They made love twice more during the night, in between talking and napping. At dawn Cord slipped out of the bed, waking Billie as he went. He kissed her softly. "It'll be better if my car isn't here in the morning," he said. "You know how small towns are."

She was touched that he would worry about her reputation. "Will I see you later?" she asked as he tucked the covers around her.

Cord gazed down at the flushed face with mussed

hair. She was warm and naked beneath the covers, and he was already hard again thinking about her. "Don't worry," he said. "You won't get rid of me that easy." He kissed her softly before grabbing his shoes and making his way from the room.

EIGHT

The flowers arrived before noon, a dozen yellow roses interspersed with baby's breath and Queen Anne's Lace and stuffed into a massive crystal vase that was impressive in itself. The arrangement looked as though it had been snatched from the main lobby of the Hyatt Regency. Billie was in the front office searching for a patient's file when the delivery man carried them in, causing quite a stir in the waiting room. Nurse Bradshaw accepted the flowers, then frowned when she read the card. "They're for you, Dr. Foster, but it doesn't say who they're from." She gave Billie a suspicious look. "But Cordell Buford has called twice asking for you, so I reckon I can put two and two together."

"Mr. Buford called *me*?" she asked, the muscles automatically tensing between her shoulder blades for reasons she wasn't quite sure of.

"Uh-huh. He didn't tell me who he was, but I've known that boy all his life, and I'd recognize that deep voice in a busy bus station."

"Did he leave a message?"

The older woman shook her head. "I told him you were with a patient. I reckon he wants to thank you for having dinner with him Friday night." She paused when Billie's mouth dropped open. "Don't look so surprised, Doctor. You can't spit in this town without everybody knowing about it. I hope you know what you're doing. Talk has it Cord's got him a new girl."

"Mr. Buford and I are just friends," Billie said as casually as she could manage. It unnerved her to know the gossip had started so quickly. The small glow that had warmed her since she'd wakened that morning turned cold. She was a doctor, a *professional*. Her reputation had to be above reproach. She could not afford to be labeled Cord Buford's latest conquest.

"Whatever you say, Doctor." Nurse Bradshaw didn't look convinced.

At two o'clock one of the mill workers came in complaining of a cough and chest pains. "You must be Mr. Buford's fiancée," he said.

Billie almost dropped her stethoscope. Anxiety spurted through her. "Fiancée?"

The man was suddenly overtaken by a spasm of coughing that brought tears to his eyes. Billie handed him a tissue and waited for the attack to subside. "Folks say it's serious this time," he went on. "They say Mr. Buford has been struck right in the heart with Cupid's arrow."

Billie tried to disguise her shock and anger with a look of total disregard. "Mr. Buford and I are *not* engaged, and I can't imagine how such a rumor got started." The man didn't look any more convinced than Nurse Bradshaw had. Billie listened to his chest, then asked about his other symptoms. "What do you do at the mill?" she asked after he'd described them to her.

"I'm a weaver."

"How long have you had this rash?" She pointed to his chest, where a patch of red had begun to creep toward his collarbone.

The man shrugged. "I hadn't noticed it, to tell you the truth. I've been doing yard work this week. Maybe something bit me, and I didn't realize."

"Just sit tight for a minute," she said. "I'd like Dr. Barnaby to have a look."

Billie found the old doctor in his office reading a file. He frowned when he saw her. "What's going on between you and Cordell Buford?"

She colored fiercely. "Is that all you people have to talk about? And when did my private life become so important to everyone?"

He went on as though he hadn't heard, snatching his spectacles off his nose. "I didn't even know the two of you were seeing each other," he said. "Now, it sounds as though you've become a real item."

"I assure you we haven't," Billie told him, her embarrassment and frustration growing to even greater proportions. "I simply went out to dinner with him Friday night. No big deal." She wasn't about to tell him the rest of it, which included Cord staying the night at her place. "Could you look at a patient for me?" she asked, deciding it best to change the subject.

"Why? What's wrong with him?"

"He's from the mill. Looks like a case of bronchitis."

"So? Tell him to drink sassafras tea for a few days and fix him up with a mustard plaster—"

"I think it's more serious than that," she said, interrupting him as he began to list the ingredients needed to make a thick paste for her patient's chest. "You remember we had three others from the mill not long ago? Well, two of them don't seem to be getting any better. This man is also complaining of headaches and dizziness."

"What's your point?"

"I think they're getting sick at the mill."

"Nonsense. That mill is as clean as this clinic."

"I know it sounds hard to believe. Bill Crenshaw, the plant manager, told me the same thing."

"You called Bill Crenshaw? Without discussing it with me first?"

"I only asked him a couple of questions," she said. "I wanted to make sure the employees were following standard safety procedures and that there had been no accidents."

"I hope you didn't make any accusations," he said sharply. "The Bufords have been good to this town."

"I haven't accused anybody of anything yet, Dr. Barnaby."

"What do you mean, *yet*?" He glowered at her.

"*Somebody's* responsible for these people getting sick," she told him, her own mood veering sharply toward anger. She was not going to back down as she so often did. "Don't you think it's a coincidence that only the weavers are getting sick? Maybe it's something in the fibers. They're not required to wear dust masks." Even as she said it, she couldn't imagine how mere dust was causing the symptoms.

He stood, giving her a look of pure, unadulterated hostility. "You know what I think? I think you are frustrated because you haven't been able to make an accurate diagnosis. Maybe you need to look through your old schoolbooks."

Fury almost choked her. Why did he insist on challenging her knowledge and skills as a physician? "My diagnosis of bronchitis is accurate, Doctor," she said, her voice sharp with rancor. "The only thing I *don't* know at this point is what's causing it."

He almost bellowed his reply. "It's not our job

to find out how and where every patient contracted his ailment."

"It is when they don't respond to medication," she replied just as loudly. "And when other symptoms appear that do not correlate. It's as though their systems are being poisoned." The shock of actually saying what she'd only been thinking up till then hit her full force. Hives, wheezing and difficulty breathing, and facial swelling such as she'd seen on one of her follow-up appointments were all symptoms of poisoning when they appeared simultaneously and when no other causes could be found. Nevertheless, poisonings involved a lot of guesswork unless the actual source was known.

Dr. Barnaby studied her for a long moment in brittle silence. "You haven't said anything to anybody else, have you?" he asked.

Billie shook her head, "I thought I should discuss it with you first."

He looked relieved. "That's the first intelligent thing you've said since you entered my office." He handed her the file he'd been reading when she'd come in. "There's a family in the waiting room needing inoculations for a trip to Japan they plan to take in a few weeks. I'd like for you to check on what they have to have and give it to them."

"But what about the patient in room one?"

"Why don't you let me worry about the patient in room one?" The old doctor gave her the closest thing he'd ever given her to a smile. "Sometimes a fresh eye is helpful."

Billie got the distinct impression he was trying to placate her. But why? "What about the others?" she asked. "They aren't responding to treatment."

"I'll take over their cases as well."

"But, Dr. Barnaby—"

"That's all," he said abruptly. When she hesitated, he went on. "Last I heard, I was still in charge here."

Billie was still pondering the change of circumstances when she finished inoculating the family of four for their trip abroad. She walked into the small cubbyhole that was her office and closed the door. She immediately went to the telephone, picked it up, and dialed the number at the plant. "I need to speak to Cord Buford, please," she said when the receptionist answered. "This is Dr. Foster from the clinic." She was put through right away.

"Billie, darlin'!" Cord sounded glad to hear from her. "I was wondering when you were going to return my calls."

"I have to see you, Cord," she whispered into the receiver.

He chuckled. "Well, that's the kind of thing I like to her."

She blushed. "That's not what I meant," she said quickly. "It's business."

"Is something wrong?"

"I hope not. Can you come to my place for dinner?"

"Sure."

"And one other thing. There are all sorts of rumors flying around about the two of us. I'd rather people not know we're seeing each other."

He was quiet for a moment. "You're not having regrets about last night, are you?"

"I simply don't want other people knowing my business, Cord." She paused. "We can talk about it tonight, okay?"

"Yeah, sure." On the other end of the line, Cord hung up the phone. He was no longer smiling.

Cord arrived promptly at seven and pulled Billie into his arms roughly, almost knocking the large wooden salad spoons she held to the ground. "I missed you today," he said, pressing a hard kiss on her mouth. "Let's get naked."

Billie, who was in the process of putting a salad together, protested lightly as he pulled her into the bedroom and kicked the door closed behind him. "What about dinner?"

"Later." He was already trying to untie her apron. He took the salad spoons from her and studied them. "I like a woman who's inventive in the bedroom," he said.

She chuckled. "They're for the salad, silly." She

tried to look serious as he pulled her apron free and started unbuttoning her blouse. "We really do need to talk."

He silenced her with a long kiss. When he broke it, they were both trembling. "We'll talk afterward," he said, the look in his eyes telling her how much he wanted her. He pulled her blouse off and gazed at the lacy bra she wore. He didn't say anything until he had removed all her clothes. Then he held her for a moment. "I love the way you smell. And taste," he added, leaning down to kiss her belly. He raised up, meeting her gaze once again as he unfastened his belt.

Their lovemaking was less hurried than the first time but no less passionate. Cord kissed her all over, waiting until she'd climaxed twice before filling her with his body.

"I'm crazy about you, Doc," he said as he shuddered in her arms.

Afterward, Billie gazed at the ceiling thoughtfully, not wanting to spoil the mood but needing answers to the questions that nagged her. "Did you tell somebody at the mill we were seeing each other?" she asked.

Cord raised up on one elbow and looked down at her. His black gaze raked boldly over her. "I don't discuss my personal life with anybody. Why do you ask?"

"Word on the street has us engaged," she said.

"Somebody must've spotted my car in your driveway last night. I was afraid of that." He smiled sympathetically. "I'm sorry. In this town sleeping together is the same as becoming engaged."

She was tempted to ask him how many fiancées he'd had, but she didn't. "I wish you'd told me beforehand," she said.

"I didn't figure you'd let a little gossip bother you."

"It bothers me very much when it affects my professional life."

"Oh, the pitfalls of small-town life," he said.

She was irked by his casual attitude. "You act as though it doesn't bother you."

"I'm used to it," he said. "But don't worry. Tomorrow the gossips will be talking about someone else." He saw that his words had done very little to appease her. "Could be you're ashamed to have your name linked with mine," he said after a minute.

"I don't need the notoriety of being labeled Cord Buford's latest conquest, if that's what you mean."

"Do you want me to stop coming by?"

"I didn't say that," she said, becoming more flustered by the moment.

"You can't have it both ways, Doc."

"I don't want people thinking I'm only looking for a bed partner while I'm here," she said, finally voicing what she'd only been thinking up till then.

He studied her closely. "But *isn't* that what you want?" he asked.

She bristled, and her face flamed a bright red under his searching look. "Of course not." He obviously had no idea how many years she had been celibate. "I want everything that comes with an intimate relationship. I want the caring and the trust and the support."

"You forgot to mention the part about being monogamous."

"Of course it'll be monogamous. That should go without saying."

"Okay. How about the commitment? I thought commitment was supposed to be a big deal with you women."

"We've already been through that."

"You mean the part where you're only going to be here for a couple of years?" When she nodded, he went on. "A lot can happen in two years, Doc."

"I have no intention of living in Ruckers, Georgia, and working with Dr. Barnaby any longer than I have to," she said, remembering her latest quarrel with the old doctor.

He pondered it. "Okay, so maybe I'll go with you when it's time for you to leave. It'll mean a lot of travel back and forth to the mills, but I can do it if I have to."

His suggestion took her by complete surprise. "Don't you think we're rushing things a bit?" she managed to ask. "We don't even know if it's going to work out between us. We're very different, you know."

"Is that so bad?"

"It is if you're thinking about spending your life with someone." She shook her head and raised up, pulling the sheet with her. "This is all happening too fast, Cord. I don't even know what I'm going to do with the rest of my life. If Dr. Barnaby keeps on the way he has, I may end up changing my name and leaving the country next week."

"I can deal with Barnaby," he said.

"No!" Billie almost shouted the word. "I don't want you fighting my battles for me. I'm a big girl; I can take care of myself. I always have."

He saw she wasn't about to back down on that subject, and he let it drop for the time being. "So, you think I'm rushing you, is that it?"

"Yes."

He thought about it. "Okay, I'll back off and go a bit slower if it'll make you feel any better." Without another word he climbed off the bed and reached for his clothes.

Billie watched him, trying to read the look on his face as he stepped into his underwear, but it was impossible to know what he was thinking. "Are you upset with me?" she asked softly.

He shrugged on his jeans and regarded her. "It's been a long time since I've cared for anybody. Since

I've given a damn about anything," he added. "This relationship obviously means more to me than it does to you."

A tense silence enveloped the room as he continued dressing. His expression was devoid of the warmth and humor that seemed such an integral part of his personality.

"Cord, I wish you'd try to understand my situation," she said.

He sat on the edge of the bed and reached for his shoes and socks. "I'm listening."

His voice was edged with an icy indifference, and Billie couldn't help but wonder if he was trying to mask his disappointment.

"My father had a heart attack six months ago. He almost died sitting at the kitchen table. He's better now, but we have no way of knowing if he'll have another." She fought to keep her voice steady. "I didn't want to come here. I wanted to be near him in case—" She paused. "In case it happens again."

"Couldn't you arrange to be sent someplace closer to your family?" he asked.

"I turned down the first two job offers. This was the third selection. I was afraid not to take it. I can't afford to pay the government back."

"How much do you owe them?"

"Thousands, why?" She looked at him. "No, I'm not asking you for the money, Cord, and I wouldn't accept it if you offered."

"Why not?"

"It means a lot to me to succeed on my own. I'm trying to make you understand how anxious I am to do what I was sent here to do so I can—"

"Get the hell out of here," he finished for her.

"Yes. I never intended to get involved with anybody."

"So why did you?" he demanded. When she looked startled, he went on. "Why did you, Billie? Were you just plain horny?"

Her face flamed. "I was lonely. Is that so hard to understand?"

"So you used me so you didn't have to be lonely anymore?"

"I wasn't using you." She got up and reached for her own clothes. "I wanted to be with you as much as you wanted to be with me. But I wasn't counting on this."

"You weren't counting on my wanting more from a relationship because you didn't think that's the kind of guy I was, right? What am I, some good-time-Charlie to get you through the next couple of years?" Even as he said it, Cord couldn't believe the words coming out of his mouth. He was used to being on the other side of this sort of argument.

"I don't think I *considered* anything," she confessed. "I'm not some great manipulator. It sort of happened between us." Dressed in bra and underwear, she walked around the bed. "I'm trying to be honest with you, Cord. So we don't misunderstand each other."

"What do you want from me, Billie?"

"For starters, I'd like your friendship."

Friendship was the last thing on his mind. He was already hard again, but how could he hope to be any other way with her standing there in her undies, looking sexier than any woman had a right to. "You got any cold beer?" he asked, although the need to escape the scantily clad woman and her sweet-smelling bedroom was greater than his thirst.

Billie nodded. "I bought a six-pack when I knew you were coming for dinner."

Cord left the room, heading into the compact kitchen and toward the refrigerator, where he pulled out a bottle of beer. He twisted off the top and took a swig. Women! Who could figure them? He'd been running from the *C*-word most of his adult life. Now, here he was looking for some kind of commitment from the feisty little doctor, and she was using many of the same excuses he'd used over the years to avoid it. Except for the part about her father, of course. If the man's health was as perilous as she made it sound, then she would resent the time she was forced to spend away from him. He shook his head sadly. Wouldn't it be just his luck to fall for a woman who wouldn't or couldn't return his feelings?

Billie walked into the kitchen a few minutes later fully dressed and found Cord sitting at the small table, leaning back in the chair with his long legs crossed at the ankles before him, a thoughtful expression on his face. He'd already drunk most of the beer, but he turned down the offer of a second. She set a plate of cheese and crackers before him, and he looked up.

"What did you want to talk to me about?" he asked.

Billie grabbed a diet soft drink from the refrigerator, slipped a pan of lasagna in the oven, and turned it on. She took the chair opposite him and wondered how to begin. "Remember I told you I'd examined a couple of weavers from the mill?" she asked, deciding it was best to jump right into it. He nodded, and she went on. "Neither of them seem to be responding to treatment. I saw a third one in my office today. He was complaining of chest pains. They all seem to be suffering from bronchitis, but I've noticed other symptoms that don't have anything to do with an inflammation of the bronchial tubes."

"Like what?"

"All three have a rash on their chests and stomach. The man I saw today was complaining of dizziness and headaches. Dr. Barnaby checked him as well. Once he left for the day, I peeked at what he'd written in the patient's file."

"Go on."

"It seems Dr. Barnaby questioned the man at length and found him slightly disoriented and confused. I'd never met this patient before, so I knew nothing of his personality. Dr. Barnaby must know him well, because he picked up on something."

"He didn't discuss it with you?"

"No. But then he doesn't usually discuss his cases with me." She smiled wryly. "Ours is a difficult relationship to understand."

His smile was just as wry. "Sort of like the one you and I have, right?" When she didn't answer, he went on. "What do *you* think is wrong with these men?"

"Honestly?"

"Of course honestly. Do you think I want you to lie to me?"

"I think they are being poisoned somehow."

Shock rendered him speechless. "How?"

"That's the part I haven't figured out. They're obviously not eating or drinking anything poisonous, because if they were, they'd have burns or sores in their mouths."

"And you think it's happening at the mill?"

She shrugged. "Where else could it *be* happening? They live at different addresses. I even asked them about their hobbies. They don't bowl together or go to the same church. Nothing."

"What did Barnaby say?"

"In a nutshell, that I should mind my own business."

"So what do you want from me?"

"Aren't you the least bit concerned?"

"Sure I'm concerned. I even talked to Bill Crenshaw after I'd found out you called him. He assured me the mill was operating at the highest safety standards, and that there had been no accidents." He paused. "But if it would make you feel better, we can both meet with him first thing in the morning."

"Could we do it at lunch instead?" she asked, knowing Dr. Barnaby would be suspicious if she came in late.

He nodded. "I'll pick you up at twelve sharp. I'll even take you on a tour and go over the safety procedures I personally implemented."

"Thanks, Cord." She smiled, feeling more relaxed over the situation now that she had his support. "I hope you're not offended by this."

"Not at all." He glanced at his wristwatch and stood. "Well, I think I'll hit the road, if you don't mind."

She stared back in surprise. "What about dinner? I have a whole pan of lasagna in the oven. It's almost ready."

"I think I'll take a rain check, if you don't mind," he said, already making his way to the door. "It's been a long day, and I'm tired."

Billie stood and followed, trying not to let him see how disappointed she was, and how vexed. It didn't make sense that he would leave before he ate the meal she'd spent two hours preparing. "Cord, is something wrong?"

He turned and smiled. "Nothing that a good night's sleep won't cure. If you'll remember, neither one of us got much last night." He leaned over, pressed a kiss to her forehead, then let himself out the door. The last thing he saw was her bewildered expression.

Twenty minutes later Cord pulled in front of his house. He suspected he'd hurt Billie's feelings by leaving so abruptly, but it couldn't be helped. He had a lot of thinking to do, mostly about her and his feelings toward her. He would have to back off, plain and simple. Otherwise, she would continue moving in the opposite direction. He couldn't risk it.

It was shortly after eleven o'clock when Billie called her parents, knowing the rates dropped after that hour. She spoke briefly with her father, then talked at length with her mother, who assured her he was doing well and following his diet.

"Did you get my letters?" her mother asked.

"All three of them." Her mother wouldn't spend money on a long-distance phone call when she could say the same thing in a letter for twenty-nine cents. Billie called them at least twice a week, but her mother refused to talk long because she thought it too expensive. "They made me homesick," Billie confessed.

"How are you liking your job?" her mother asked.

"It's wonderful," Billie told her. "I'm meeting so many nice people." She tended to sugarcoat things since she felt her parents had enough to worry about with finances and her dad's heart condition. She didn't want to add to their problems.

"I'm sure the other doctor is glad to have you," Martha Foster said, the pride in her voice almost drawing tears from Billie. "Honey, we need to talk about the money you sent last week."

"I'm not going to argue about it, Mother." Billie sounded stern. "Now that I'm making money, I expect you to let me pay you back."

"But you don't owe us anything, darling, and besides, you have other debts."

"I'm doing fine." Billie wasn't about to confess how she'd pinched pennies to send them the amount she had. She figured it was the least she could do. Although her parents had never had a lot of bills, she wanted her mother to pay off whatever ones existed in case her father got sick again.

"Your father wouldn't like it," her mother whispered from the other end of the line. "He's a proud man, Billie. Why, if he even suspected you were sending us your hard-earned money—"

Billie cut her off. "We had a deal, Mother. You promised."

"I'm not used to keeping things from your father."

"It's for a good cause," Billie told her. "We both know how important it is to keep him from worrying. One way to accomplish that is to pay off all your bills."

"I make pretty good money in my cleaning job, you know."

"I want you to save that. You may need it to fall back on."

Her mother was silent for a moment. "Okay, sweetheart," she said at last. "You're the doctor, and you know what will help your father get better. I hope you're not having to sacrifice more than you should. You still have to pay rent and buy groceries."

Billie laughed. "I've already told you, they supplied me with a cute little apartment here. And the ladies from the nearby church are always bringing goodies into the office for me to take home. I'm probably going to be fat before long." She could hear the smile in her mother's voice when she spoke.

"I'm so glad you're happy, and that your life is going well. This is what we worked for, remember?" She didn't give Billie a chance to answer. "Now, hang up the phone before this bill gets to be more than you can afford."

"Good night, Mom. I love you." Her mother made kissing noises on the other end before she hung up.

Billie was still smiling as she undressed for bed, but it was a sad smile of longing and missing the people she loved most. She thought of Cord and grew sadder, wishing he hadn't left so abruptly. Perhaps she should have tried harder to make him understand why it was impossible to build a life in Ruckers. She climbed into bed, grabbed a magazine, and tried to read it. Talking to her parents had made her lonelier than ever. She thought of calling Cord but decided against it. It wasn't fair to need him one minute and send him away the next.

Finally, she switched off her light and closed her eyes.

NINE

Cord was waiting for Billie when she stepped out of the clinic a few minutes after twelve the next day. She sensed, as he drove toward the mill, that he was as uncomfortable as she was. She didn't know if it had to do with the business at hand, their personal relationship, or both. He parked his car near the front entrance and led her inside the building to an office down the hall from Bill Crenshaw's. "What time do you need to get back to the clinic?" he asked her as he motioned for her to take a chair on the other side of his desk.

"Two o'clock." Billie glanced at the tidy office, trying to discover more about the man before her. Although it was tastefully decorated, there were no personal artifacts, no family photographs, nothing. It could have belonged to anybody.

"I thought I'd go over our safety procedures, then

take you on a tour of the mill," he said, reaching for a manual on the walnut credenza that matched his desk. When she nodded, he went on. "It's really very simple. By law, our employees have the right to know exactly what chemicals, hazardous or otherwise, we use, as well as the risks involved in case one is ingested. We employ our own safety manager, who travels to each mill and sees that we are in compliance with all regulations. He couldn't be here this afternoon because he's giving a training program at another site. But since I'm the one who created his job, I can answer all your questions."

Billie nodded and listened as he outlined the comprehensive training program that each employee was expected to complete before being assigned to a department.

"Each supervisor has a copy of this manual," he said. "It lists safety rules such as how a container is supposed to be labeled so that it is clearly identifiable and contains the appropriate hazard warning. This manual also gives the toxicity levels of each chemical, the precautions one should take when using the chemical, and first-aid procedures in case someone comes in direct contact. You'll notice that we've also listed the departments that use certain chemicals." He handed her a sheet. "This lists each chemical used in the weave room. None are extremely hazardous. And this—" He paused and handed her a folder. "These are copies of our Material Safety data sheets for the past six months. You can take them with you if you like. You'll notice that none of the chemicals used in our area have been changed or altered in all that time."

"Which means?"

"Which means we are still buying the exact same chemical from the same manufacturer, so there's absolutely no reason to believe these illnesses are chemically induced." He handed her yet another file. "These are copies of workmen's compensation claims filed by our employees over the past year."

Billie took the file and looked through it, recognizing Dr. Barnaby's familiar scrawl as the attending physician. There was a back sprain, a cut hand because an employee was negligent with a piece of machinery, and various other minor injuries that were almost not worth mentioning. Nevertheless, each injury was listed, as well as the treatment that had been provided. "We are proud of our safety record," Cord told her when she closed the file. They spent another half hour in his office before he led her on a tour of the mill. Finally, he led her into the weave room, where more than two hundred looms were being operated. He nodded and waved to various employees as he tried to talk above the noise, and Billie couldn't help but notice the curious stares she received.

"We don't require dust masks in the weave room because we take other precautions to see the dust level is safe," Cord told her. "Notice how moist the air is in here?" When Billie nodded, he pointed toward the ceiling. "If you'll look closely, you'll see tiny jets protruding from those horizontal pipes along the ceiling. Each jet spits out a fine mist. It's our way of purifying the air." He went on to explain briefly the weave process itself, the dangers involved no matter how minor, and the emergency procedures taken in case of an accident. By the time he led Billie back to the executive offices, she felt she'd learned more than she would ever remember.

Bill Crenshaw looked delighted to see Billie and made quite a fuss over her, seeing that she had a cup of coffee and was comfortably seated before they began their meeting. "I understand we have problems," he said, his tone becoming serious.

Billie told him about the lack of progress the weavers were making healthwise and saw the news had him genuinely concerned. "I want to run blood tests on them," she said. "But they're going to want to know why."

Crenshaw nodded as though he fully understood. "It's their right to know."

Cord cleared his throat. "I'm not sure that's a good idea, Bill. They might panic. Who knows what sort of rumors would fly."

"Better to start a few rumors than have them suspect we're keeping things from them," the other man said. "Besides, we have nothing to hide."

"What if some government agency gets wind of

it?" Cord said. "They'll want to investigate. They might even close the place down while they do it. Think how it would hurt our employees. Most of them live from one paycheck until the next as it is. Besides, you know how my father would react to any bad press concerning one of his mills. It would embarrass the hell out of him. He likes to think we're setting standards for other mills."

Bill Crenshaw seemed to ponder it. "I've been friends with Art Buford long enough to know that he'd want this looked into despite the chance of rumors or bad press."

Cord gave a snort. "Then you obviously know him better than I, because I think he'll have a stroke over it."

"You can't let your personal feelings for your father cloud your professional judgment of him," Bill pointed out gently.

Cord pondered it, then turned to Billie with a heavy sigh. "Okay, let me play devil's advocate here for a moment," he said. "Suppose you discovered the mill was indeed responsible for our weavers getting sick. I'm not saying we are, but let's play 'what if' for a moment. What's your next step?"

"I'd have to report it," she said. "Your employees would be entitled to workmen's compensation. Who knows, Workmen's Comp. might start their own investigation." She looked from Cord to Bill Crenshaw as she spoke. The older man seemed to be taking the news well enough. Cord was the one having problems. If he was so sure the mill wasn't responsible, why was he worried about people finding out?

"When do you want to draw blood from the weavers?" Bill asked.

"Right away. Before their conditions worsen."

"Can you give me time to talk to my old man first?" Cord asked. "He went out of town this morning, but I should have no problem finding him."

"Certainly." Billie was thankful they were moving in the right direction. She offered the men the closest thing she had to a smile. "I'm sorry for all this," she said softly. "I wish none of it had happened."

"So do we all," Crenshaw said. "But if something *is* going on in this mill, I, for one, want to know, and I don't care if the entire country finds out."

Cord didn't echo that sentiment. He stood, shoved his hands deep in his pockets, and headed for the door. "You'll be hearing from me," he told Billie before he made his way out.

Bill Crenshaw stood, bringing the meeting to an end. "He's upset right now, but he'll get over it," he said, nodding toward the closed door where Cord had exited. "We think of the mill workers as family, and it distresses us if someone becomes ill. I'm afraid Cord's assessment of his father is fairly accurate, although I don't want to admit it to the boy."

"What do you mean?" Billie said, standing as well.

"Art has changed over the years. He used to care about his mills and the people who work in them. Now, he only sees the bottom line, the profits. He wasn't always like that."

"You and Mr. Buford have been friends for a long time, haven't you?"

He nodded as he walked Billie to the door. "I started at the bottom and worked my way up. Art must've seen promise in me, because he's worked me in just about every department over the years. Accounting, engineering, personnel, even the lab, if you can believe it. Ten years ago he made me plant manager." He paused as though remembering it all. "Yeah, Art and I go way back. You know, it was me who introduced him to his wife. I was there the night Cord was born, and I can't remember a Thanksgiving or Christmas that I wasn't included. I guess I sort of think of them as flesh-and-blood family."

"Then you obviously know Cord blames his father for his mother's death," she said, then wondered if she'd said too much.

The man's face clouded. "He *was* to blame," he said, his voice suddenly mournful yet tinged with anger. "He killed her as surely as if he'd put a gun to her head." He squared his shoulders then and offered her a smile that belied the harsh words. "Have a good day, Dr. Foster."

Dr. Barnaby was none too happy to discover how Billie had spent the afternoon, and he said as much the minute she walked through the front door. "I told you to drop it," he said, "but you refused to listen. Have you forgotten that it is because of the generosity of the Bufords that we have this clinic to begin with?"

"I haven't forgotten," she said, wondering how the news had gotten back to him so quickly. "But I'm not going to turn my head to the fact that we are treating three of their employees for what looks like a work-related illness."

"Four," he said, tossing a file on her desk.

Billie blinked. "What?"

"Another one came in this afternoon. A woman who works as a weaver. Says she's been sick two weeks now with a chest cold. Also complaining of headaches and dizziness."

Billie was almost hopeful. "Does this mean you believe me now?"

"I don't know what to believe anymore," he muttered, "except that I'm getting too old for this sort of thing. I can't for the life of me figure out what's wrong with these people."

Billie was touched by the small confession. "Well, if it makes you feel any better, neither can I."

He glared at her. "I didn't tell you that to gain your sympathy, Doctor. And just because I agree with you in this one particular instance, I don't want you to think you've swayed me over to your way of thinking or that we'll develop some sort of friendship."

"I never suspected it for a moment," she said softly, doing her best not to grin. "We'll never be best buddies."

For a moment it looked as though he might smile as well. "Just as long as we understand each other. Now I suggest we get them back in here for a blood test."

"I agree completely," Billie said in her most professional voice.

The men and one woman were tested the following day. After drawing their blood, Billie had the samples hand-delivered to the laboratory in the next town to await results.

"Something's wrong at the mill, isn't it?" the middle-aged woman named Kay Nettles asked Billie as soon as Billie finished with her.

"What makes you say that?" Billie asked, trying not to answer one way or the other.

"Mr. Buford questioned us all yesterday afternoon. He asked if there had been any accidents in the weave room. I can't think of any sort of accident that would make us sick like this."

Billie decided she would try to be as honest as she could without giving away more information.

"Frankly, we don't know if this has anything to do with the mill or not," she told the woman. "We're investigating all possibilities. I expect we'll know more in a couple of days."

The woman looked anxious. "I hope it's nothing serious. I'm raising two grandchildren."

"I'm sure it's not, Mrs. Nettles," Billie said, although there was no way she could know one way or the other.

The blood-test results came in two days later. Negative. Dr. Barnaby tossed the lab report onto Billie's desk and waited until she'd finished reading it before saying anything.

"Satisfied?" he asked.

"Of course not," she told him. "We still don't know what's making these people sick."

He gave a snort of disgust. "Well, at least we know what's *not* making them sick. I only hope the Buford family doesn't decide to sue our socks off."

"I seriously doubt the Bufords would take us to court over something like this," she said only a split second before he walked out of the room.

Billie was still trying to make sense of the negative blood tests when she left the clinic at five-thirty and made her way across the backyard toward her apartment. Cord was sitting on the top step. "What are you doing here?" she asked. "Did you come to gloat?" She regretted it the moment she said it, regretted further her tone of voice.

"Gloat?" he asked as though he couldn't quite figure out what she meant.

"I'm sure Dr. Barnaby informed you of the blood-test results."

"He called this afternoon."

"Well, congratulations." She tried to step past him.

"Billie, wait—" Cord stood, grabbed her wrist, and pulled her to a stop. "I came because I knew how upset you'd be, because I knew how much you were counting on these tests to tell you what is making these people sick. I'm sorry you're not any closer to finding out."

She pulled free, blinking furiously in an attempt not to cry. While she'd had no desire to implicate Buford Textiles over the illnesses, she desperately wanted to know what was making Kay Nettles, grandmother of two, sick. Not to mention the men, all of them hard workers with families. "I'd think you would be relieved over the news." She unlocked her door and shoved it open.

"Then you don't know me very well. Sure, I hate to think these people are getting sick at my mill, but I'm as determined to find out what's wrong with them as you are." He paused when she stepped through the door. "Mind if I come in?"

Billie shrugged and held the door open for him to

pass through, then closed it behind him. "You want a cold beer?"

"Sure." He followed her into the kitchen and watched her take out a beer and a diet soft drink. He accepted the beer with a brief thanks before joining her at the small kitchen table.

"You haven't come around," she said after a moment.

"You asked me to back off."

"Are you sure that's the only reason?"

"This business with the mill has nothing to do with us. Besides, I would have come by sooner, but I had to go out of town for a couple of days." He saw her look soften. "Am I forgiven?" She shrugged, and he grinned. "So who's on call tonight?"

"Dr. Barnaby. I don't think he trusts me with his patients anymore since I made such a big fuss over the mill workers. If that weren't bad enough, he said he ran into Gus Jennings at the drugstore and Gus told him I had absolutely no business practicing medicine. At the moment I'm beginning to think he's right."

"Barnaby will get over it. And so will you."

She wasn't convinced. "The sad thing is, I think Dr. Barnaby was starting to believe in me."

"And now?"

"It's clear I've embarrassed him."

Cord reached for her hand and squeezed it reassuringly. "It'll pass, Billie. In the meantime you can't sit around feeling sorry for yourself. Let me take you to dinner."

"The last time I went to dinner with you, folks started shopping for our wedding gift."

"Which is why I'm taking you to a restaurant in the next town," he said. When she looked surprised, he chuckled. "See? I've thought of everything. Now stop arguing with me and get dressed."

They were on their way twenty minutes later. The Peddler Steak and Chop House was almost forty-five minutes away, but the time passed quickly as Cord and Billie chatted and listened to a Garth Brooks tape. By unspoken agreement they didn't discuss the mill, the strange illnesses, or her job at the clinic. By the time they arrived at the cozy restaurant that resembled an oversized log cabin, Billie's mood was much improved.

Cord ushered her through the front door and into a waiting area where a large, old-fashioned meat case dominated the room. "See, you get to select your steak right here," he said, motioning to the window where thick cuts of steaks and chops were displayed. "I highly recommend the filet mignon."

They were seated a moment later. Billie spied a tall frozen-strawberry daiquiri on a nearby table and decided to order one. It arrived shortly afterward, topped with whipped cream and a plump strawberry.

She said it was the best she'd ever had. They ended up ordering the filet mignon. Cord waited until their waiter left them before he said anything.

"Glad you came?" he asked Billie as she licked whipped cream from one corner of her mouth.

"Definitely."

"Sometimes I feel like getting away," he confessed. "This is where I come. It's not too far, but it's far enough to make me feel as though I'm taking a temporary vacation away from my troubles." He gave her a small smile. "I've been here a lot the past year."

"Do you think it has helped?"

He nodded. "I'm not as angry as I once was. In the beginning I was consumed with hatred for my father. The only person I could really talk to was Bill Crenshaw, but even that was difficult."

"Because he was so close to your father?"

Cord shook his head. "No, because he was in love with my mother." When Billie arched both brows, he went on. "Bill was engaged to my mother before he introduced her to my father. My father wooed her with flowers and fancy restaurants. They'd only known each other two weeks before they took off for Vegas for one of those quickie weddings. She was still wearing Bill's engagement ring at the time. I think she regretted it almost instantly, but it was too late. She got pregnant with me on their honeymoon."

"Is that why Bill Crenshaw never married?"

Cord shrugged. "I haven't asked. But I can tell you this. He never got over losing my mother, nor she him."

"Didn't it affect his and your father's friendship?"

"At first. But my old man continued to offer him one promotion after another. That's the way my father is. He thinks he can buy everything and everybody."

"It must've worked. He and Bill are friends again."

"I guess that means everybody has their price," Cord said, his expression wry. He was quiet for a moment, speculating. "I suppose that's why I've always gone after what I wanted," he said, giving her a long look. "Otherwise, you risk losing it."

Billie was still pondering their conversation when they arrived back at her apartment shortly after ten o'clock. "Would you like to come in?" she asked, once Cord had walked her up and unlocked the door for her.

He studied her. "You know I would. But I've got a meeting first thing in the morning. I was wondering if you're on call this weekend."

"It's Dr. Barnaby's turn, why?"

"I have to go to North Carolina tomorrow to check on one of the mills. We could have dinner and spend the night."

She wanted to go in the worst way. Despite the fact that she was afraid of becoming more involved with him, despite the fact that she still hadn't discovered what was making the mill employees sick. "I have to work at the clinic until noon. After that I'm free for the rest of the weekend."

He kissed her lightly on the lips. "I'll see you tomorrow afternoon."

TEN

Cord arrived at Billie's apartment shortly after noon on Saturday and found her frantically rushing to get ready. He followed her into the bedroom, where she grabbed a small suitcase from a shelf in her closet. In her haste she knocked a shoe box over, dumping a pair of new heels onto the floor.

"Hey, slow down," he said, bending over to retrieve the shoes. "We aren't in that big a hurry." He returned the dainty heels to the box and stuffed it back in the closet, pausing at the door when he caught the faint scent of her perfume. His gut tightened as he remembered smelling it on her cool skin.

Billie tossed him an apologetic look. "I'd planned to pack last night," she said, "but I never got the chance." She told him about the accident involving a church bus with thirty people on board. "Dr. Barnaby had to call me in to assist. We didn't leave the clinic until after three."

"I heard about it this morning," Cord said, sitting on the edge of her unmade bed and trying not to think of her in it. "Was anybody seriously injured?"

"We sent the driver to the hospital with a fractured wrist, but most of the injuries were minor. We stayed because another bus had to be found to take the passengers home." She hurried over to her dresser and opened a top drawer, grabbing panties and bra. She tossed them into the suitcase, then fumbled through several other drawers for socks and pantyhose and her nicest nightgown. She turned to put them in the suitcase and found Cord fingering a tiny strip of lace on a pair of underwear. She blushed profusely at the sight, then tossed the other items on top. "Should I pack anything special?"

"No, this is fine."

She threw him a stern look. "I can't very well spend the entire weekend in my underwear."

He grinned. "Yes, you can."

Their gazes met and locked. She had trouble breathing when he looked at her that way. His bandage was gone, and his forehead was healing nicely. He had never looked more handsome and virile than he did at that moment. "Pervert," she replied, trying to make her voice sound light despite her nervousness, despite the thickening tension in the room. She grabbed a pair of socks from her suitcase and threw them at him playfully.

Cord ducked, but not fast enough. The socks hit

him squarely in the face. "You shouldn't have done that," he said, his tone low and seductive. "Now, you'll have to pay."

Billie took a step back, feeling certain her friskiness had been brought on by a bad case of nerves. Cord's voice, with its underlying warning, sent a ripple of awareness through her. The almost feral look in his eyes made her stomach quiver. With the speed and agility of a large jungle cat, he lunged for her. She squealed and tried to get away, but she was not as quick as he. He hauled her up, flailing arms and all, and carried her to the bed, where he dumped her unceremoniously. She tried to get up, but he shoved her down, lost his balance, and fell on her. She struggled in vain to get up. "Cord!" she said, laughter bubbling up from her throat. "Get off me!" He silenced her with a kiss.

Billie stopped struggling the moment his mouth came down on hers. All rational thought ceased to exist, and she was held immobile by the sheer intensity of it all. He forced her lips apart with a thrusting tongue, then sank it deep inside. The kiss deepened and became hungry. When he finally broke it, they both gasped for air.

He gazed into her eyes, his breathing as labored as if he'd just run a race. "I want you," he said. "Here and now."

Billie's stomach took a nosedive. She answered him by moving closer. Her skirt crept up her thighs.

He saw it as an invitation and plunged one hand beneath it, impatient to touch her again, to taste her. He struggled with her pantyhose, cursing the individual who had invented them. In his haste he stuck a finger clean through a leg. His black eyes beseeched her. "Help me get these damn things off, and I'll buy you a case of them."

Billie couldn't help but laugh as she peeled off the now-ruined nylon stockings. They'd barely had time to hit the floor before her underwear fell beside them with a whisper. Without wasting another second, Cord shoved the skirt higher and buried his face in the dark brown thatch of hair that covered her femininity. Billie closed her eyes and arched against him, crying out softly. He clutched her thighs, holding her fast, his mouth devouring her as if she were made of the sweetest nectar.

Desire sent her blood racing through her body like a turbulent river, lifting her on a hot tide of passion. She rose, higher and higher, then crested, and her whole being flooded with desire. It was white-hot. Earth-shattering. She grasped his head, crying out in a moment of uncontrolled passion. It rose, subsided, and rose again. And then he left her for a moment. Billie opened her eyes and found him kicking off his shoes and stepping out of his clothes. The look on his face took her breath away.

When he returned to her, he was naked and hard and more magnificent than any man she'd ever seen.

He swept her legs apart. Poised over her, he met her gaze for one electrifying moment before thrusting deeply inside her. It was a raw act of possession. A moan of sheer ecstasy slipped from her throat and passed through her lips. He caught it with his own lips as he moved against her, slow and deliberate. Their paces quickened, and once again Billie was caught up in a place where nothing else existed but feeling and sensation. They peaked, and his own orgasm followed a split second behind hers. The world spun out of control, and they clung to each other as though half-afraid they would fall off. They shuddered together, then drifted back to earth.

They were on their way forty-five minutes later, after taking a quick shower and dressing. Instead of taking the interstate, though, Cord passed it. "I know a shortcut," he told Billie when she glanced at him in question.

The shortcut turned out to be a single-engine Cessna parked beside a small airstrip outside the city limits. Cord parked his Corvette beside a fiberglass building that served as both hangar and office.

Billie looked at him. "Someone is flying us to North Carolina?" she said.

"Me."

"You fly?"

"No, but my plane does." He saw that she didn't

look amused. "Relax, I've had my pilot's license for years."

"You didn't tell me we were flying to North Carolina."

"You didn't ask."

"You *should* have told me, Cord. Flying makes me nervous. Flying in *that* is going to make me doubly nervous."

"There's no reason to be nervous, Billie," he said, turning slightly in his seat to face her. "Traveling by airplane is much safer than traveling by car."

"Then how come you never hear of Lincoln Continentals going down in some cornfield on the eleven o'clock news?"

"Trust me," he said, getting out of the car. He walked over to her side and helped her out, then reached into the back for their luggage. "Besides," he added with a grin, "there are no cornfields nearby."

"*That* is supposed to make me feel better?"

He set the luggage down next to the plane and ushered her inside the building. "I need to file a flight plan," he told her. "You might want to visit the ladies' room before we board."

Billie was still nervous when he helped her inside the plane a few minutes later. Cord tucked their suitcases in back, then assisted her with her seat belt. "Why do I need a seat belt?" she asked. "If we crash, I'm going to be dead whether I have it on or not."

"We're not going to crash, and you need it in case we hit an air pocket."

"If we hit an air pocket, I'm going to wet my pants."

He chuckled as he fastened his own seat belt. "No, you're not. That's why I made you go to the ladies' room before getting on."

Billie was still fighting a case of bad nerves as they taxied down the airstrip and waited for permission to take off. Cord looked very much at home in the cockpit, setting dials and flipping switches with those same brown hands that had caressed her little more than an hour before. He moved with an air of confidence, answering whatever questions she had in a voice that sought to reassure. Nevertheless, Billie didn't breathe a sigh of relief until they'd left the ground and leveled off. Cord reached for her hand and squeezed it.

"That wasn't so bad, now was it?"

Billie pulled her hand free. "Please keep both hands on your instruments," she said.

"I'd rather have my hands on *your* instruments." He saw that she was in no mood for teasing. "Okay, okay," he mumbled. Following his flight plan, Cord headed east, flying directly over the Okefenokee Swamp before turning due north. The plains became a gently rising plateau, skirted by a purplish mountain range in the distance. Before long they were flying directly over the Blue Ridge Mountains. Awed by the sight, Billie forgot her nervousness. "It's beautiful," she said. She turned to Cord and found him watching her, a warm smile on his face. She wondered if he had any idea what that smile did to her. She felt her insides turn to mush.

"I knew you'd like it. This is another way I escape."

As they flew—actually, Billie decided it was much like floating, since they didn't seem to be moving— Cord pointed out various sights. When they landed a couple of hours later, Billie declared it had been the smoothest flight she'd ever taken. She even looked forward to the return trip. Cord grabbed their bags, checked in at the office, and led her to an older-model Jeep waiting in the parking lot.

The drive to the mill didn't take long. "Are you sure you want me to come along?" Billie asked when she realized they were going to the plant. "I don't mind waiting at the hotel."

He shook his head. "There's something I want you to see."

"Oh?"

He didn't quite meet her gaze when he answered. "I should have told you in the beginning," he said, "but I didn't want you to say anything to anybody."

"Should have told me what?" she asked. When he hesitated, she became insistent. "Cord, what's going on?"

"I need your opinion," he said. "As a physician."

"On what?"

"A few people have gotten sick at this mill. I want you to tell me if you think they're suffering from the same sort of illness as those in Ruckers."

Billie gazed back at him as he turned into the parking lot. "I didn't bring my medical bag."

"I don't think you'll need it. From what I understand, the symptoms are similar. Wheezing and coughing. Headaches and dizziness. A couple of them have a rash."

"I don't know, Cord. I'm sure they have their own family doctor. He or she might not appreciate me stepping in."

"All I want is your opinion, Billie," he said, "based on what you've seen at the other mill. I don't expect a formal report."

She nodded after a moment. "As long as we understand each other."

The patients, one man and two women, sat across the conference table from Billie and Cord and answered various questions about their symptoms. Billie made notes on a legal pad. One of the women confessed to having a small rash above her left breast. "Do all of you work in the same department?" Billie asked.

The man nodded. "We're weavers."

Cord and Billie left the mill a couple of hours

later, each wearing a perplexed frown. Neither of them spoke until they were back in the Jeep and on their way.

"You're going to have to do something, Cord," Billie told him. "These people are eligible for workmen's comp. The mill should be paying their medical bills."

"Even though we don't know what's wrong with them?"

"But we *do* know it's somehow work-related." When he didn't say anything, she went on. "You *do* know that?"

"I don't know what the hell to believe anymore."

"What does your father say?"

"He doesn't want it leaked out. I came up here against his wishes." He sighed. "But it's not fair to shroud this whole matter in secrecy because we don't want bad press or because we don't want to involve the federal government. People are getting sick. For all we know, this thing could kill them."

"What are you going to do?"

"What am *I* going to do?" he repeated. "Well, as soon as we get back to Ruckers, I'm going to close down the weave room for a couple of days and go through it with a fine-tooth comb. My old man will have a fit, of course, but it won't be the first time we've butted heads. One way or the other I'm going to find out what's making these people sick." He looked at her. "In the meantime, though,

I'm going to try and get it off my mind so we can enjoy ourselves. Do you like ice cream?"

The change of subject was so abrupt, it surprised her. "I love it, why?"

"Hang on tight, I know just the place."

The ice-cream parlor was located along a narrow cobblestone street in a shopping district where old houses had been transformed into art galleries, souvenir stores, and antique shops. The entire city was flanked by mountains. Billie ordered a double-dip of chocolate fudge, and Cord ordered something with chunks of walnuts. They licked their ice cream as they made their way past the various shops, stopping every so often to peer into one of the windows. The temperature had dropped considerably, and Billie was surprised how cool it was for the last week of June.

"Which hotel are we staying in?" she asked Cord once they'd climbed back into his Jeep and pulled onto the road.

"We're not staying in a hotel."

"Another surprise?" she asked, thinking of the small airplane that had brought them there.

"My mother's family was from this area. They left their house to her when they died. She used to come out whenever she could. Now, I use it."

The house turned out to be a small brown-shingled cottage tucked away on a mountain road. Billie had to smile when she stepped inside the living room where the white wainscoted walls and plump floral sofas gave the place a homey, lived-in look. "I love it," she said, following Cord into a kitchen where built-in cupboards only added to the feeling of nostalgia and warmth. Cord set two bags of groceries down on a marble pastry table on which a pitcher of wildflowers sat.

"The cleaning lady must have picked them from out back," he said when Billie leaned over to smell them.

Billie smiled. "Thank you for bringing me here, Cord. It's wonderful." She paused. "Do you mind if I look around?"

"Make yourself at home," he told her. "I'll join you as soon as I put these things away."

"Now, I know why we had to stop at the grocery store," she said. "You're not likely to find any fast-food restaurants way up here."

He chuckled as he opened the refrigerator and put a carton of milk and juice inside. "That's why I like it."

Billie spent the next few minutes exploring the house. The master bedroom was as quaint as the rest of the place, with its old iron bed and pine cupboard that served as a bureau. Across the hall she found the bathroom to die for, complete with a vintage porcelain tub. She heard Cord come up the stairs behind her. "I guess you know where I'll be spending all my time," she said, nodding toward the tub.

He slipped his arms around her waist and pulled her flush against him, then leaned over slightly so he could nibble on an earlobe. She shivered as the skin on the back of her neck prickled. "It's big enough for two," Cord said, his warm breath fanning her as he spoke. He turned her around and kissed her fully on the lips. It was a slow and thoughtful kiss, made sweeter by the fact that he took his time. When he pulled free, he smiled down at her. "Let's get into something comfortable and take a walk. I want to show you around."

Ten minutes later they left the house wearing their oldest jeans and sneakers. Billie had donned a short-sleeved cotton blouse as well, and he a simple Polo. Holding hands, they started down a dirt road flanked by woods.

"If I lived out here, I would never want to leave," she told him.

He smiled down at her. "Maybe we won't."

"I couldn't do that to Dr. Barnaby. He'd miss me terribly."

Cord squeezed her hand. "Give him time, he'll come around."

She chuckled. "You don't believe that, and neither do I."

They had only walked a short distance before Cord directed her through a path in the woods that led to a spot on the edge of the mountain that overlooked a deep valley. Standing behind her, Cord slipped his arms around Billie's waist. They stood there for some time, gazing at the majestic mountain range that would have inspired the most hardened soul. "It's breathtaking," Billie said, loving the feel of Cord's arms around her.

He kissed the back of her neck. "So are you."

"I am?"

"Didn't you know that? You take my breath away."

"You're a sweet-talker, Cord Buford."

"And when we come back next fall, we'll be able to build a fire in the fireplace."

"Next fall?" She turned around and regarded him, her expression quizzical. "Aren't you filling my date card a little far in advance? I hope this doesn't mean you're already taking me for granted."

He squeezed her tight. "All it means is that I won't allow you to see other men."

She nuzzled the V in his shirt where his chest hair curled against his open collar. "I love this masterful side of you," she teased.

"I may as well tell you I'm the jealous type," he confessed. He crooked an index finger under her chin and tilted her head back. Her eyes sparkled like emeralds. Finally, he captured her lips and kissed her deeply. He heard her stomach growl, pulled back slightly, and laughed against her mouth. "Does that mean you're hungry?"

"Mountain air and good lovin' always make me ravenous."

"Don't tease me, Billie," he warned, running his hands across her pert behind, "or I'll have to turn you over my knee."

She grinned, broke free, and took a step back. It was dumb to feel this sappy about a man, but she did. "You and what army, Cord Buford?" Her tone challenged him.

He approached her slowly, his stride purposeful. "You're acting mighty cocky, shrimp."

"Shrimp!" Billie drew herself up to her full five foot two inches and regarded him sternly, hands on hips. "Just who are you calling a shrimp, buster?" Her bravado was shattered as he lunged for her. She managed an inarticulate squeak before he hauled her up and threw her over his shoulder. "Put me down, Cord Buford," she cried, noting that, while the position was definitely awkward, she had a clear, undistorted view of his backside. The snug jeans emphasized his tight, well-muscled behind.

"Nope. I'm taking you home with me, little lady."

"Is this the way you mountain men treat women?" she asked, struggling to no avail. She would have had more luck swimming against a fast-moving current.

"That's right," he said, taking to the narrow mountain path once more. "We see a woman we like and we throw 'em over our shoulder like a sack of potatoes. If you ask me, women and potatoes are good for only one thing."

Still dangling from his shoulder, Billie tried to imagine what that might be. "The only thing you can do with potatoes is—" She swallowed the rest of the sentence as a rosy blush stained her cheeks and crept upward. "Cord!" She kicked her legs. "You're terrible"

He chuckled. "You got a dirty mind, shrimp, you know that?" He put her down. "Think you can walk the rest of the way?"

"I'm beginning to think I'd better run," she told him, still a bit embarrassed by his comment.

"You ain't goin' nowhere, Doc," he told her, his drawl thick as maple syrup.

Billie's cheeks flamed, and she tried to think of a way to change the subject. Her solution came thirty seconds later when she gasped and came to an abrupt halt only a few feet from a rock on which a large snake had decided to take his afternoon nap. "Cord?" His name was a whispered croak.

Cord saw the snake the same moment she did. He froze, put his arm out to stop her, then relaxed when he saw that it was not the deadly coral snake he'd thought at first. He had seen enough of the so-called "Louisiana snakes" in these mountains to recognize the orange, black, and white pattern that so often made people think it was the poisonous variety. This snake was perfectly harmless.

Not that he had any intention of telling Billie that.

"Don't move," he said.

Billie couldn't have moved if someone had put a gun to her head. She was literally paralyzed with fear.

She tried to speak. "Is it . . . ?"

"Yes, it's very dangerous," he whispered. "But don't worry, I'll save you."

Too afraid even to move her head, Billie cut her eyes in his direction. "How?"

"I'm going to throw my body on him while you run." The horrified look she gave him convinced Cord he was a real creep for doing what he was doing. Still, he couldn't resist, knowing how grateful she'd be later.

Panic rioted inside her. "No, Cord. I can't let you do that."

"A man does what he has to in order to protect his woman, Billie."

She was touched to the core by his words and the tender look on his face. "You really *do* care that much?" she asked. "Enough to die for me?"

He was so overcome with guilt that he knew he couldn't continue to lie. "It's not poisonous, Billie," he said, nodding toward the snake, which was watching them now.

"Don't lie to me, Cord. I know a coral snake when I see one."

"It's not a coral, Billie. I swear," he insisted when

she continued to look doubtful. "I let you think that because I wanted to appear brave. He's actually harmless. And obviously stupid, or he wouldn't just sit there." He stepped closer to the snake. As though deciding the human had finally ventured too close, the snake slithered off in the opposite direction, disappearing into the brush. Cord turned and found Billie watching him, a curious smile on her face.

"Was that true?" she asked. "What you said just now?"

"You mean about lying to you?" he asked, looking somewhat embarrassed. "I suppose that makes me a jerk, huh?"

"Not that part, silly," she said, feeling suddenly shy. "The part about protecting your woman. I thought guys only said those sorts of things in old westerns."

"Yeah, I meant it," he said. "I suppose you're ready to run as fast as you can in the opposite direction."

She smiled gently, her heart bursting with affection for the man who looked as though he were only moments from ducking into the brush the way the snake had. She knew she was very close to being in love with him. Or perhaps she already was, and she was fooling herself out of fear. Fear of committing herself to a life that did not fit into her plans and to a man who would probably end up breaking her heart. She thought she detected a flicker of apprehension in his eyes, and it occurred to her for the first time that he was as anxious as she was about what was happening between them. Finally, she took a deep breath.

"I'd be lying if I told you I wasn't afraid of my feelings toward you," she said at last. "But I've never run from anything in my life, and I'm not about to start now."

He wanted to take her in his arms, but his own doubts made him reluctant. She had not really revealed that much, and he was terrified of laying his heart open when he was so unsure of her feelings. He would have given all he owned to know where he stood with her. "So what now?" he said. "What will you do with me now that you've got me wrapped around your little finger?"

Billie's heart lurched madly at the thought that he might indeed care for her as he claimed. She stepped closer and put a hand against his cheek. He was so devastatingly handsome that she had trouble thinking when she looked at him. His black eyes impaled her. He was trying to read her feelings. Why couldn't she tell him how she felt? All she had to do was place his open palm against her chest and prove that even her heart beat faster when he was near.

She was a coward, she decided, when the words didn't come. Instead, she stepped closer and put her arms around his waist. "I'm going to take very good care of your feelings, Cord," she said softly. "I promise."

It was not exactly what he wanted to hear, but he knew it would have to do for now. "I can live with that," he said, taking her hand and pressing a kiss into her open palm. "At least for the time being."

Holding hands, they left the woods behind and made their way down the dirt road once more while Cord reminisced about the summers he'd spent playing in those same woods as a child. "My grandparents were simple, down-to-earth people. Some of the happiest times of my life were spent here. Then, after my grandfather died and my grandmother had a stroke, my mother insisted she live with us." He gave Billie a sad smile. "The poor woman hated leaving this place."

"How did your father like having his mother-in-law under the same roof?" Billie asked.

Cord shrugged as he led Billie up the driveway to the house. "I wouldn't know," he said. "My father has never shared an emotion in his life."

Billie was still thinking about what he'd said when they entered the house a few minutes later. Cord rummaged through the refrigerator for salad greens and put them next to the sink. "I hope you're a good cook."

She thought of the lasagna that she had prepared for him, sitting in her freezer now. Had he not left in such a hurry, he would have found out for himself that she wasn't half-bad in the kitchen. But she didn't say anything. To bring it up would only emphasize the fact there were troubled areas in their relationship that neither of them were ready to face. "I do okay in the kitchen," she said after a moment.

He looked relieved. "I grill a mean steak, but that's the extent of my expertise in that department."

She smiled sweetly. "Good thing for you that I enjoy cooking. The bad news is, I hate cleaning up afterward, and I noticed there's no dishwasher."

"I reckon I'll have to pitch in."

She took the lettuce and unwrapped the plastic covering. "I reckon you will."

He smiled at her. He couldn't recall a woman ever telling him he was going to have to wash the dishes after he finished eating. Usually, they were only too happy to clean up while he stretched out on the sofa. "Do you think you can stay out of trouble while I go find the grill?"

"I'll try."

He started out the door and paused. "Oh, and don't forget to put the potatoes in the oven to bake. You know how I love potatoes."

ELEVEN

Once dinner was finished, Cord helped Billie clean the kitchen and put a pot of coffee on to perk.

"Tell you what," he said, folding a dish towel and draping it over the sink. "You run a bath, and I'll bring us up a cup when it's finished."

"That's nice of you."

"I'm a nice guy."

She kissed him lightly on the lips. "I'm beginning to think so myself." He patted her on the fanny when she turned to go.

Billie made her way up the stairs and into the cozy bathroom, where she turned on the old-fashioned faucets. She noticed a jar of bath oil nearby and couldn't resist. Later, she sighed her immense pleasure as she sank into the lilac-scented water. She closed her eyes and leaned against the tub, feeling more relaxed and happy than she had in a long time.

She knew, in her heart, it had everything to do with the man downstairs.

By the time Cord entered the bathroom with two coffee mugs, Billie was on the verge of falling asleep. He paused inside the door and gazed at her for a long silent moment. She had never looked lovelier or more desirable, and he had never cared for a woman as much. He stepped closer. His ears roared when he looked down into the tub. Her skin was slick; her breasts glistened from the oil that laced the water. Her eyelids fluttered open.

"You're not falling asleep on me?" he asked, his voice deceptively calm. He realized he was trembling when coffee sloshed over the side of one cup and burned his hand. He set the coffee cups down on a small table beside the tub. If Billie noticed his discomfort, she didn't say anything.

"I've never felt so relaxed in my life," she confessed, trying to talk around a wide yawn.

He smiled at her, retrieved a footstool from near the sink, and placed it beside the tub. "Must be all this mountain air and good lovin'," he said, that teasing look back in his eyes. He reached for a large sponge. "But you can't fall asleep before I wash you."

Something inside of her leapt to life. "Wash me?" Her voice quavered.

"That's right." He sat on the stool, dipped the sponge into the water, and worked up a lather using one of the bars of specialty soaps his mother had kept on hand before her death.

He started with her feet. They were dainty, the arch clearly defined. Her toes were pink, the nails painted a deep coral. He soaped them, top and bottom, sliding his brown fingers between her toes as she giggled like a young girl and tried to pull her foot free.

He chuckled. "You never told me you were ticklish."

"You've never washed my feet." She was thankful when he started up her slender ankles and calves. Finally, he moved past her knees to her thighs. Billie sucked her breath in sharply when he discarded the sponge and rubbed the soap back and forth across the dark thatch of hair at the V of her thighs, creating a thick white lather. She arched against the palm of his hand, parting her thighs slightly. He saw it as an invitation, slipped his fingers between them, and explored. She inhaled sharply at the contact, then moaned softly when he dipped one finger inside her moistness.

Cord watched her face closely as he slowly but expertly caressed the satin lining, making gentle forays with his finger while flicking his thumb lightly across the sensitive bud that never failed to arouse her. Her face was flushed, her breasts stained pink with desire. He took his time with her, building her to climax gradually, deriving as much pleasure as she by just watching her. It was like watching a flower bloom through a time-lapsed lens. Finally, she cried out in a moment of uncontrolled passion.

When Billie opened her eyes, she found Cord watching her, a tender expression on his face, his hands resting on the side of the tub. She was filled to bursting with an amazing sense of completeness. At the same time she felt drained of all physical strength.

"Aren't you coming in?" she asked.

Cord didn't miss the weariness in her voice. "Not tonight, sweetheart," he said. "I think you need sleep more than anything." When she tried to apologize, he hushed her. "We have tomorrow." Cord stood and reached for a towel. "Here, stand up, and I'll dry you."

Billie stood so he could assist her. All at once she couldn't stop yawning. "I guess I didn't get enough sleep last night," she said, feeling as though someone had tied tiny weights to her eyelids. She finished drying while Cord fumbled through her suitcase for a gown.

The sheets were crisp and cool when Billie climbed between them. "What time is it?"

"Eight o'clock."

"How embarrassing."

"That's okay, mountain people go to bed early. That's why they have so many kids."

She smiled and closed her eyes as he tucked the

covers around her. She was asleep before he left the room.

When Billie opened her eyes again, it was morning. She blinked several times as she took in the quaint bedroom, then smiled when she remembered where she was and who the big hairy arm belonged to that was draped over her. She turned over and found herself looking into Cord's handsome face. He was sleeping soundly, his black hair mussed, his lips slightly parted. She lay there for a long time, watching him, listening to his steady breathing, and wishing she never had to leave the haven of his embrace.

The thought of returning to the clinic and Dr. Barnaby depressed her, but she knew she had to go back. Perhaps now that she'd had a chance to get away, she could be more tolerant of him and his criticism. Billie climbed out of bed, taking care not to wake Cord. She made her way to the bathroom, where she was immediately reminded of the way her bath had ended the night before. Something fluttered in the pit of her stomach as she remembered Cord's hands bringing her to orgasm, then lovingly tucking her into bed. She washed her face at the sink and dried it on a hand towel. She tiptoed down the stairs to the kitchen and put a pot of coffee on the stove to perk. She had just poured a cup when she heard Cord come down. She grabbed another from the cupboard and filled it.

He stopped inside the doorway. "Good morning. Did you sleep okay?"

He was dressed in pajama bottoms, bare from the waist up, his unshaved jaw giving him a rakish look. Billie suddenly felt awkward in her nightgown. "Better than I have in months. Sorry I pooped out on you last night."

"You needed the rest." He took the coffee cup she offered. "Want to sit on the front porch and drink this?"

"In our pajamas?"

"Who will know?"

She laughed. "Pardon me, I forgot where I was." She followed him out to the porch, where they sat in tall rockers and sipped their first cup of coffee. The mountain air was fresh and cool on Billie's face. Birds chirped in a nearby tree. "You know, if more people lived like this, we'd have fewer heart-attack victims in this country."

He tossed a quizzical look in her direction. "You're saying this is good for my heart?"

"Absolutely."

He reached for her hand and squeezed it. "So are you, Doc," he said. "You're damn good for my heart."

She met his black-eyed gaze. "You're good for mine too. As long as you don't break it."

"And you think I will?"

She stirred uneasily in her chair, wishing now she hadn't made the comment. "The thought has crossed my mind."

Setting his coffee cup down, he reached for her. "Come here."

Billie set her cup down as well, raised up from the rocker, and stood before him. He parted his bent knees and encircled her with his arms, resting his hands on the back of her thighs. He pulled her close, pressing his face against her flat stomach. She smelled of soap and woman. Cord tilted his head back and gazed into the face he'd come to love in a short time.

"I won't hurt you, Billie," he said, his eyes riveting her to that spot. "I care for you too much." He paused and gave her a slight smile. "You, on the other hand, could rip my heart out with your teeth if you wanted."

She was touched by his honesty, by the stark vulnerability she saw in his eyes. She knelt before him and laid her head against his thigh. It was warm and slightly muscular. He stroked her hair, and she was lulled into a feeling of peacefulness and contentment by his touch. He was obviously not as relaxed, she realized when he began to squirm in his chair. He had, in a brief period of time, become aroused by her nearness. Billie smiled and gazed up at him, her eyes sparkling with deep affection for the man before her.

"As I recall, we have some unfinished business left over from last night," she said.

He arched one dark brow. "We do?"

She gave an emphatic nod as she reached for the fastening of his pajama bottoms. He sucked his breath in sharply at her touch. "Oh, Mr. Buford," she said, using her professional voice. "We seem to have some sort of growth here. A very *large* growth," she added, slipping her hand inside and closing her fingers around his hardness. She caressed him, and he moaned. "Is it giving you any trouble?" she asked.

He chuckled and leaned his head back in the chair. "It is *now*."

She inched his pajamas down. "Well, since I don't have my medical bag with me, I reckon I'll have to take matters into my own hands, so to speak."

His look of surprise turned to astonishment. "Here? Now?"

"Who will know?"

The flight back to Ruckers was uneventful, which meant it was a good flight as far as Billie was concerned. Night had fallen by the time they landed. Cord tossed their luggage into the trunk of his Corvette, and they headed back to Billie's place. He parked his car in the garage beneath her apartment so as not to start more gossip. Once inside her cozy living room, they kissed one another deeply.

"I had a great time," he told her.

"Me too."

He continued to hold her. "I should go. It's getting late."

She tightened her grip on him. "I don't want you to go," she said, feeling closer to him than ever. They had formed a bond in the mountains that was stronger and more intense than any she had ever experienced with another man. "We could make popcorn and watch television together," she suggested.

He stroked his jaw as if in thought. "I don't know, Doc. This is beginning to smack of commitment, what with spending two nights in a row together. You know how nervous that makes you."

He was teasing her again. "Is that a yes or a no?" she said, tilting her head back in order to see his face.

He pressed a kiss against her forehead. "I could never say no to you, Billie Foster."

She kissed him back, then led him into the bathroom, where they showered together, taking great delight in washing each other. Afterward, they dried and put on their pajamas. "You see what's on TV, and I'll make the popcorn," she told him.

They ended up watching an old spy movie of which Billie understood very little, forcing Cord to explain the plot as they went along. "Are we watching the same movie?" he asked when she continued to get confused with what was happening.

"This is why I don't like this kind of movie," she said. "I never know who the bad guy is."

"So what kind of movies do you like?" he asked.

"Thrillers. I'm a big Hitchcock fan. I've seen all of his movies at least three times."

"Now, I know what to get you for your birthday," he said, making a mental note. He frowned. "By the way, when is it?"

Billie began cleaning up their popcorn bowls and soft-drink cans. "Not for six months. You have plenty of time to shop." She dumped the leftover popcorn into the trash and yawned. "I don't know about you, but I'm tired."

"I'm ready to go to bed too," he said, stretching and yawning as well.

For some reason she suddenly felt shy with him. She wasn't accustomed to having a man sleep over, and she was certain it showed. "You can brush your teeth first if you like. I'll turn the covers down on the bed."

Cord nodded and went into the bathroom. He could tell Billie was feeling a little awkward about his staying, and he was determined to make it as comfortable for her as he could. They had spent a wild and wonderful weekend in the mountains, but now they were back to the real world of jobs and alarm clocks. He had problems at the mill; she had problems at the clinic. They had been careful not to mention their problems all weekend for fear of spoiling the mood, but the following day they would have to face them all over again. Still, he could not think of anybody else he'd rather share those small drudgeries with.

"It's all yours," Cord announced, coming out of the bathroom a few minutes later.

Billie nodded and hurried in to brush her teeth and apply moisturizer to her face. When she came out, she found Cord standing beside the bed. "What's wrong?" she asked, wondering why he hadn't climbed in.

"I was wondering which side you like to sleep on."

"The side facing the bathroom."

"Good, that means I get to sleep closer to the air conditioner. I get hot during the night."

"Which explains why you kicked all the covers off the bed last night," she said. She reached for the alarm clock, started to set it, then glanced his way. "Is six-thirty okay?" she asked. "I like to get up and read the newspaper before I go in."

He nodded and climbed in on his side, feeling stiff and unnatural. "Six-thirty is fine."

"One or two pillows?"

"One."

"I use two." She switched off the lamp and lay down, pulling the covers to her chin. Neither of them moved. "Uh-oh," she said, sitting up abruptly.

"What is it?"

"I can't sleep with the door open." She climbed out of bed, closed the door, and hopped back in. "In case of fire," she said. "My parents taught me always to keep my bedroom door shut." She shut off the light.

"That's good." He turned on his side facing her and slipped one arm under his pillow. He was just about to reach for a kiss.

"Uh-oh."

"What now?"

The lamp came back on. "I forgot to turn the radio on the easy-listening channel." She raised up once more and switched on the radio on her night table. "I sometimes have trouble falling asleep. Do you?"

He yawned wide. "Not until tonight. Is there anything else?"

She paused. "If I tell you, you're going to think it's really dumb."

"Try me."

"See the small fan on your bed table? I usually turn it on low."

He glanced in the direction of the fan. "Why do you need a fan when the air conditioner is running?"

"The sound puts me to sleep."

He considered it. "But how can you hear the fan running with the radio on?"

"Trust me, I'll know if it's not on."

He sighed, raised up on one elbow, and reached for the switch on the fan. "Okay, how's that?"

"Perfect."

"How about the television set?" Her sudden case of nerves was making him anxious as well. "You want me to drag that in here too?"

"No, I can't sleep with the TV on."

"Good night, then," he said, snuggling under the covers once more.

"Good night." Billie switched off the light and lay down as well. "Uh-oh."

"No!" he almost bellowed. He reached for her in the darkness and dragged her the few inches that separated them. He sought and found her mouth and kissed her hard.

It wasn't until then that Billie realized she was acting like a nut. What was wrong with her, for heaven's sake? Nerves, no doubt. She simply wasn't used to having a man in her bed. She kissed Cord back, suddenly tickled with herself for what she'd put him through. Laughter bubbled up from her throat.

Cord pulled away abruptly. "What are you laughing at?"

"Me. Us. I'm driving you crazy, aren't I?"

"That's it, Billie. I've had it." He whipped the covers off the bed.

She groped for them in the dark. "What are you doing?"

He literally fell on top of her. "I'm going to make love to you," he said. "And when I'm finished with you, you won't need the fan or the radio or all that other stuff to fall asleep, 'cause I'm going to wear you out."

At first Billie thought the banging noise was a dream, then she realized someone was knocking on her door. She snapped awake when she realized it might be an emergency. Quickly, she slipped out of bed, wanting to see to the knocking before it woke Cord, who was already stirring restlessly beside her. She opened her bedroom door and hurried out, flipping on the hall light as she went. She crossed the room and paused at the door long enough to pull the curtain aside. She gasped out loud.

Her parents!

Billie was so stunned, at first all she could do was stare through the windowpanes at the frantic faces of her mother and father.

"Open the door, Billie," her father said impatiently from the other side.

Billie unlocked the door and swung it open. Her mother rushed through and took her in her arms. "Thank God you're okay!" she said, enveloping Billie in the smell of talcum powder.

Still dazed, Billie watched her father step through the door. "What are you two doing here?" she asked.

Charlotte Hughes
170

Her father regarded her, his face masked with concern. "Your mother has been trying to call you all weekend," he said in the same voice he'd used on her when she was sixteen years old. "When we couldn't get you, we called the clinic. The other doctor said he hadn't seen you since Saturday morning. We even had the police come by and knock on your door. They said your car was in the driveway, but you weren't answering the door."

"Naturally, your father suspected the worst," her mother said.

"Me?" he replied, raising his voice. "*You're* the one who insisted she'd hit her head in the bathtub and drowned."

"Billie, why haven't you answered your phone, for pete's sake?" her mother asked.

"I was out of town," she said, wishing her father would not get that worried look on his face that always made her think he was on the verge of another heart attack.

"Out of town?" they replied in unison.

"Daddy, you need to calm down," she said. "You know what your doctor said about letting yourself get so upset. It's not good for you."

"My daughter disappears off the face of the earth," he said, "and I'm not supposed to worry."

Billie was about to respond when she heard the bedroom door open. Her parents snapped their heads up simultaneously and stared as Cord came into the room, rubbing his eyes.

"What's all the commotion out here?" he said, still half-asleep.

Billie felt her heart slam to her throat at the sight of him in his pajama bottoms, hair mussed. She turned, dreading the moment when she'd have to look into her parents' faces. The look in her father's eyes riveted her to the spot. She was vaguely aware that Cord had come up beside her.

"Cord, I want you to meet my parents," she said, noting the news had the same effect on him as if she'd doused him in the face with ice water. She didn't have to touch him to know every muscle in his body had tensed with the news. "Martha and Joe Foster," she added, studying her father's face as she made the introduction. It was a dangerous-looking beet red.

Cord saw the situation was desperate. Billie's father looked as though he were about to stroke out. He held out his hand. "Mr. Foster, nice to meet you," he said as politely as he could.

The older man's jaw trembled. It was obvious he was having trouble controlling himself. "Who the hell are you?" he demanded, his eyes staring coldly into Cord's.

"I'm Cord Buford, sir. Billie's new husband."

TWELVE

Billie was certain that had her parents not been so shocked over the news, they would have noticed the shocked expression on her own face. She opened her mouth to say something, then closed it when the words simply wouldn't come.

"Husband?" Martha Foster said in a voice of disbelief. "When did this happen?"

Cord cleared his throat. "This weekend, Mrs. Foster. Billie and I flew to Vegas Saturday and tied the knot yesterday."

"And you didn't *tell* anybody?" her mother said, looking at Billie as though she had suddenly sprouted horns.

"I'm sorry, Mom. It was sort of spur-of-the-moment."

"Spur-of-the-moment?" her father bellowed. It was obvious he didn't think his daughter had acted responsibly.

"Mr. Foster, I know it sounds as though we acted quickly, but the truth is, I fell in love with your daughter the first time I laid eyes on her."

"And how long ago was that?" Joe Foster asked. "She didn't even tell us she was seeing anyone."

"Cord and I have been seeing each other since I moved here, Daddy," Billie said. "He went out of his way to see that I felt welcome in this town. We've spent almost every free minute we have together. I wanted to be sure he was the one before I said anything."

"And are you?" her father asked.

"Yes. Cord is the man I want to spend the rest of my life with."

"What about your career?" he asked. "All the money and hard work to get through medical school?"

"I support Billie's career one hundred percent," Cord interrupted. "I'm very proud of her."

Joe Foster looked at his wife. "I need a drink of water."

Martha Foster went into action. "Have your father sit down, Billie," she told her daughter, "while I get him something to drink."

"Allow me," Cord said, hurrying toward the kitchen. When he came back, the Fosters were sitting on the sofa. Billie had taken the chair opposite them. "Here's your water, sir," Cord said, handing Billie's father a glass. Nobody said anything until he was finished with it.

Martha Foster seemed to feel as though she needed to calm her husband. She faced Cord. "I'm sorry if my husband and I appear rude," she said. "It's just—" She paused. "We had no idea." She looked at her husband. "But we're delighted that Billie has fallen in love, aren't we, dear?" When he merely grunted, she went on. "After all, Billie is almost thirty years old, clearly mature enough to make such a decision." She took her husband's hand in hers. "It was love at first sight for us, too, wasn't it, dear?"

Joe Foster's face softened for the first time. "Yeah, I guess so."

"And my parents thought we rushed into it, remember?" She squeezed his hand. "That was thirty-three years ago, and we're still together." She smiled at her daughter for the first time, and it was obvious that, while she needed time to adjust to the news, she couldn't risk having her husband upset over it. "We hope you'll be very happy, darling."

Billie's eyes misted, and she was overcome by guilt. Why had she let Cord lie? Why hadn't she said something? "Thanks, Mom," she managed.

Joe Foster didn't seem to be listening. He was watching Cord closely. Finally, he spoke. "My daughter means the world to me," he said.

Cord knew then that Billie's father had been devastated by his son's death and was trying to do everything he could to protect his only living child.

It touched him that the big man could love her so fiercely.

"I love her with all my heart, sir," Cord told him. "I promise to take good care of her."

Billie couldn't help but notice the weary look on her father's face. "Daddy, why don't we all get some sleep?" she suggested. "We can talk more in the morning."

"That's a wonderful idea," Martha Foster said. "Your father and I passed this little motel a few miles back—"

"Nonsense," Cord said. "We have plenty of room, don't we, honey?" When Billie merely gave him a blank look, he nudged her.

"Sure we do." She tried to sound enthusiastic. She would have preferred her parents going to a motel so she and Cord could figure out what they were going to do. "The sofa makes into a bed," she said. "You and Daddy can have . . . our bed, and Cord and I will sleep out here." A blush stained her cheeks.

"We'll be perfectly comfortable on the sofa," Martha said. "After all, this *is* your honeymoon."

"Where's your ring?" Joe Foster asked.

"My ring?"

"Your wedding ring."

Cord hurried in. "We didn't have a chance to pick out rings, Mr. Foster. We're going to do that first chance we get." He put his arms around Billie.

"We also have to plan a real honeymoon, don't we?" He squeezed her, and she forced herself to smile back at him like a devoted wife. "It isn't easy for us to get away right now with our jobs," he added, "so we've decided to wait until we can afford the time."

"What kind of work do you do?" Joe asked, obviously wanting to know how his new son-in-law planned to provide for his daughter.

"Not now, Joe," Martha said, getting up from the sofa. "We'll have plenty of time for that in the morning." She turned to Billie. "If you'll show me where your sheets are, I'll make up our bed. Joe, honey, why don't you run out to the car and get our suitcase—"

She'd barely had a chance to get it out of her mouth before Cord offered. "I'll do it," he said.

Joe handed him the car keys and waited until Cord left before saying anything. He looked directly at Billie. "You and I are going to have a long talk in the morning." Then he grabbed the Sunday paper from the coffee table and marched into the bathroom.

Billie looked at her mother. "He's never going to forgive me."

"You can't blame him for being hurt, dear," Martha said, pulling cushions off the sofa so they could open it out. "We both are. We had dreamed of giving you a nice wedding."

Guilt stabbed her. She couldn't allow the lie to continue. "Mom, there's something I need to tell you," Billie said.

The woman glanced up, obviously startled by the tone of her daughter's voice. "You're not pregnant?"

"Oh, no, it's nothing like that," Billie said quickly, then was interrupted when Cord came through the door with her parents' old suitcase. He set it on the floor.

"Billie, would you please open the suitcase and get my blue zippered pouch out?" Martha said. "I forgot to give your father his medicine." Billie nodded and opened the suitcase out on the kitchen table.

"I'm going to bed," Cord announced to no one in particular.

"I'll be in shortly," Billie told him.

Martha walked into the kitchen, where she filled her husband's water glass and counted out various pills. Billie glanced at the bottle and noted her father's dosage had been raised. "Is he doing any better?" she asked.

Her mother sighed. "I suppose so. But it's difficult to make him follow doctor's orders. You know how stubborn your father is." She smiled. "I believe you had something you wanted to tell me?"

Billie had been so concerned with her father that she hadn't noticed how weary her mother looked, how bone-tired she must be from working full time and caring for a sick husband with a heart condition. "It was nothing, Mom," she said, giving her mother a kiss on her cheek. "I just wanted you to know, Cord is a wonderful man. He'll make a wonderful husband. Please don't worry about me."

"As long as you love each other, dear," Martha said, "and from the looks of it, I think you do."

Billie kissed her mother once more, then made her way to the bedroom, passing her father in the hall as he stepped from the bathroom.

"I love you, Daddy. Good night."

Billie felt as though she'd slept only about twenty minutes when the alarm clock went off the following morning. She shut it off and lay back down, trying to figure out what she was going to do about the mess she was in.

"Good morning," the man next to her said. "Are you still mad at me?"

She shot him a dark look. "What do you think? Somehow, we have to figure a way to undo all the damage that was done last night."

He scooted closer and felt her stiffen automatically. It had been a sleepless night for him as well. Billie had refused to talk to him, and he'd heard her crying once. "I didn't know what else to do," he said softly. "Your father looked as if he would explode when I walked out of your bedroom in my pajamas.

I remembered what you told me about his bad heart, and I panicked."

"How do you think his face is going to look this morning when I tell him we aren't really married and that we slept together last night while he was under the same roof? My parents are old-fashioned people, Cord, with very high morals. They won't go for it."

"Don't tell them."

"What!"

"Look, it's not as if they live next door or even in the next town, for that matter. How often will they visit?"

"You're crazy if you think I'm going to carry on this ridiculous charade," she said, flipping the covers off so she could climb out of the bed. "Lies may slip from your tongue like honey, but I'm not accustomed to telling them."

"What the hell is that supposed to mean?"

She paused and put on her bathrobe. "It means you will say anything to serve your purpose. I can't help but wonder if what you said about caring for me is a bunch of bull as well." She knew she sounded bitchy, but she couldn't help herself, knowing what lay ahead.

He sprang from the bed, grabbed her around the waist, and pulled her back, causing the old mattress to squeak and groan beneath them. "I'll show you the difference between truth and bull," he said, grinding his mouth against hers.

"Stop making so much noise," she said, but her words were muffled with his kiss. She shoved with all her might, but it was useless.

When he raised up, he was grinning. "I'm beginning to think I might like married life after all."

"That is *not* funny," she said, her lips feeling bruised from his kiss. "Now, I know you're out of your mind, crazy as a loon."

"Be careful, Billie, darlin'," he said, still grinning. "I'm not the one who goes to sleep at night with all the appliances running."

In a huff Billie climbed out of the bed once more and stuffed her arms into the sleeves of her bathrobe. Cord slapped her playfully on the fanny as she leaned over to retrieve her slippers. The last thing she saw before she closed the door was his laughing black eyes.

"Good morning, dear," her mother said as Billie stumbled into the kitchen. Martha had already made coffee and was having her first cup. Billie glanced toward the sofa and saw that it had already been made, the covers folded neatly in a stack on the coffee table.

"Where's Daddy?" Billie asked as she headed for the automatic coffeemaker.

Martha nodded in the direction of the bathroom. "He kept me up talking half the night," she said, "but I think he's finally resigned to the fact you're married."

Guilt was beginning to leave a bad taste in Billie's mouth. "Mom, I'm so sorry," she said. "That was a crummy thing to spring on you."

Martha shrugged. "What's done is done, and Cord seems like a nice young man. Frankly, I consider it a true test of love when two people can't wait to become man and wife. I know that's how it was for your father and me."

"That doesn't mean you're off the hook, young lady," Joe Foster's deep voice said as he came into the room. "Your mother and I expected to see you get married, and we aren't about to let you take that away from us."

"What do you mean?" Billie asked.

"We decided we would go ahead and stay a couple of days longer," he began. "In the meantime we want you and Cord to find a minister who can marry you the way you should have gotten married in the first place. I don't hold much for those quickie Las Vegas weddings. I'm not even sure if they're legal." When Billie opened her mouth to object, he cut her off. "I know we won't have time for a fancy reception and all, but the least we can do is be there when you and Cord exchange your vows. It'll mean a lot to your mother," he said, as though embarrassed that a burly man like himself was making such a big deal out of something that should matter only to women. "We'll take you to dinner afterward to celebrate, then leave for home the next morning."

Billie was speechless for a moment. He'd laid it all out for her in such a way that she would have felt crummy letting them down. "I don't know, Daddy. Where am I going to find a minister who'll agree to marry us that fast?"

Martha looked surprised. "Why, I would have thought you'd started attending church by now, dear."

Billie blushed, recalling that she spent most of her Sunday mornings in bed until at least ten o'clock. "I'm still shopping around for just the right one," she said, wondering if lying was habit-forming.

Cord cleared his throat from the doorway. "I couldn't help overhearing," he said. "My family minister will be only too happy to marry Billie and me." He looked at Billie. "I would have insisted on it sooner or later, sweetheart. This Las Vegas marriage was fun and all, but I won't feel truly married until a minister pronounces us man and wife."

Billie wanted to slap him. Did he have to practice that silly charm, or did it come natural?

Tears sprang to Martha's eyes. "Oh, my, what a romantic thing to say. Isn't that romantic, Joe?"

Joe grunted and took his place at the table where his coffee had already been poured. "It would have been more romantic if they'd waited until I could give them a proper wedding. This slipping off in the middle of the night doesn't sit well with me at all. I don't even know what this man does for a living."

"Cord has a very good job at the mill in town," Billie rushed in. "Actually, he's in charge of several mills."

"In charge?" her father repeated, arching one brow.

Cord shifted uneasily in his chair. For some reason Billie was reluctant to tell her parents he had money. "It's my job to see the mills are operating efficiently, sir," he said. "I earn a decent living."

"And it's secure?" the older man asked.

"Very."

"Well, don't get too cocky, son, or you might find out that you're not as indispensable as you think." Joe took a sip of his coffee. "Now, about this wedding business. How soon can you arrange it? I have to get back to my job as well."

Cord and her parents were still discussing wedding plans when Billie left an hour later for the clinic. Dr. Barnaby frowned the moment he saw her. "Your mother called looking for you this weekend. I stopped by your place twice, but you weren't home."

"I know, I'm sorry she had to bother you. They were worried about me. They're visiting me now."

"Well, I don't have time to look after you," the old doctor grumbled. "And I'm too old to have to worry about something happening to you. How long are they here for?"

"Just a couple of days."

He gave a snort. "I suppose you'll be wanting some time off."

"No, I—"

"You can't expect to leave them in that tiny apartment all day while you work," he said. "Don't you young people ever think about anybody but yourselves?" He didn't give her time to answer. "You can take a couple of hours off for lunch, then go home early if you like."

"If you're sure you don't need me."

"I was running this place fine before you got here. I don't reckon it'll fall apart if you take some time off."

"Thank you, Dr. Barnaby." She gave him such a big smile that he quickly became flustered and left.

When Billie went home for lunch, she found Cord and her parents eating sandwiches and conversing easily at the kitchen table with the classifieds opened before them. "You didn't go to work today?" Billie asked Cord.

"I figured I'd take the day off since we had company." The way he said it, one would have thought they had been together forever. He paused, gazing steadily at her in a way that told her something was amiss. "Your parents think we need a bigger place. They've found us a house in the newspaper," he added, his low voice sounding a bit awkward.

Martha stood and approached her daughter. "Honey, your father and I don't mean to interfere, but we think this place is rather small for two people. Now, I know you probably won't start your family for a couple of years, but it wouldn't hurt to go ahead and get something a little larger. Cord feels the same way."

"You do?" Billie looked at him.

He looked from Billie to her mother, feeling caught in the middle. "I want whatever you want," he said. "But your parents are right about this place being small." He paused, looking for a way to change the subject. "Aren't you going to eat your lunch?" He motioned to a plate with a sandwich and chips on it.

Things were happening much too fast for Billie. She sank onto the chair next to her mother, took a bite of her sandwich, and decided sawdust would have had as much flavor. She pushed her plate aside. "Did you call the minister?"

Cord nodded. "After you eat your sandwich, we need to drive down to city hall for a license. I gave them all the information on the phone—all we have to do is sign the forms."

"And your minister can perform the ceremony Wednesday?" Oh, Lord, what was she saying! She was obviously becoming so involved in the lies that she didn't know truth from fantasy.

"It wasn't easy getting him to agree to everything so quickly, but yes, he can do it Wednesday evening. As long as the license is ready. I figure I'll keep pestering them at city hall until it is." He glanced at her uneaten sandwich. "If you're finished with your lunch, we need to run," he told her.

Still reeling from all that was happening, Billie hurried into the bathroom and brushed her teeth, then ran a brush through her hair. "I plan to get off work early today," Billie told her parents before she headed out the door with Cord. "I hope you won't get too bored sitting here."

"We'll be fine," her mother assured her. "We might even drive over and look at this house listed in the paper. You need almost no money down to buy it."

Billie started to object, then decided not to say anything. If her mother wanted to go look at a house, fine. That didn't mean she and Cord had to buy it. At least it would keep her parents occupied while she was gone. "I'll see you at three o'clock," she told them.

Billie didn't say anything until they were on their way. Finally, she turned to Cord. "What are we going to do now?"

He chuckled. "Damned if I know."

"This has gone too far, Cord. We have to stop it."

He drove in silence to city hall, then parked his Corvette in front of the quaint building. "Would marrying me really be so bad, Billie?" he asked after a moment.

Whatever she had expected to hear, that was not it. She stared back at him in silence. Finally, she found her voice. "Cord, have you completely lost your mind?" she asked. "We can't get married simply because we lied ourselves into a corner with my parents."

"It was a good reason to lie if ever there was one," he said. "I don't know about you, but I'll never forget the look on your old man's face when he laid eyes on me in my pajama bottoms."

"That's no reason to get married," she told him. "Marriage is a lifetime commitment."

"We could probably have it annulled as soon as they left if it would make you feel better," he said, wanting to wipe that look of despair off her face. "We'll tell them we came to our senses and realized we'd rushed into it without thinking."

"More lies," she said, heaving a heavy sigh.

This time it was Cord who sighed. He took Billie's hand in his. "Look, Billie, I guess it's no secret that I'm in love with you. I know it happened fast, but it's not something I take lightly. As far as I'm concerned, marriage would only enhance that love." At the doubtful look she gave him, he went on. "I'm sorry if you don't share that sentiment."

"I didn't say that," she told him, touched to the core by his confession of love. "It's just, I expected it to be different from this."

"You want me to propose to you?" he asked gently. "Because I will if that's what it takes."

She was almost moved to tears by the tender expression on his face. She didn't want him to propose just to get her out of a bind. "You've been wonderful, you know that? I'm not happy with the mess we're in, but I want to thank you for being kind to my parents."

"How could I not be kind to them? They gave birth to the woman I love."

Her eyes misted, and she leaned against him. Cord put his arms around her and kissed her forehead. "I love you too, Cord," she said softly.

He went still in her arms. "Are you sure?"

She nodded. "I just didn't want to admit it."

He put a finger beneath her chin and raised her head so that he was looking into her eyes. "I wanted to think you did," he said, "but I was afraid to hope for so much. You've made me take a long look at myself, Billie. I haven't always been the sort of man you'd be proud knowing, but I swear if you'll give me half a chance—" He paused and kissed her fully on the lips.

"I still think this is crazy," Billie said when he pulled away. "I should go right back and tell them the truth, that I'm almost thirty years old and plenty old enough to have an affair with a man if I want to."

"So why don't you?"

"I'm afraid my dad will have another heart attack, and it'll be my fault."

He didn't say anything for a moment. "Why didn't you tell me the brother you lost was your twin, Billie?" he asked finally, as gently as he knew how.

She swung her gaze around. "How did you find that out?"

"Your parents carry pictures. I saw all two hundred and seven of them over coffee after you left for the clinic this morning. You and your brother were the spit and image of each other. Why didn't you tell me?"

Billie glanced away. "I didn't think it was important."

"Talk about giving a line of bull," he muttered. When she looked back at him, he went on. "You wouldn't have kept it from me unless it *was* important, unless you had a reason. You blamed yourself for his death, didn't you?"

"When did you become a psychologist, Cord?" she asked tersely.

"I don't have to be a psychologist to figure it out. You blamed yourself for being the healthier twin, didn't you?"

She swallowed the lump that had suddenly appeared in her throat. "Yes, at the time I did. But I've gotten past that."

"I don't think you have. Otherwise, you wouldn't live in fear of your dad having a heart attack. I don't think it's fear as much as it is knowing you'll have to go through all that guilt again."

"My brother's death was hard for me," she said. "I'm not denying that."

"I understand he wanted to be a doctor. Is that why you became one instead?" Cord asked.

"I suppose that's what first got me interested. I knew he would never live to realize his dream, so I did it for him."

"What did you want to be?"

She looked embarrassed. "An actress."

"No kidding?"

"No kidding." She laughed and wiped her eyes. "Good thing I became a doctor instead, because I can't act worth a cuss." She laughed again. "Of course, Dr. Barnaby would probably tell you I'm not much of a doctor either."

"Do you think you're a good doctor, Billie?"

"Yes, I do. I saw how indifferent some of the doctors acted toward my brother when he was so sick, and I'm not like them. Maybe some doctors feel they have to keep a distance so they don't get emotionally involved, but if I shed a few tears over losing a patient, what's a few tears compared to a lost life? I genuinely care about my patients. That's what got me through medical school, Cord. Knowing that I could be there for somebody."

"So you don't regret it?"

"No. I would have been lousy on Broadway."

Billie checked her wristwatch and saw that it was getting late. "We'd better go in," she said. "I have to get back to the clinic."

They climbed out of the car and made their way up the steps leading to city hall. Cord squeezed her hand. "Stop acting so nervous. All we have to do is sign the forms and leave."

She paused inside the large double doors that marked the entrance. "I'm not saying I'm going through with this, Cord," she told him. "Let's take it one step at a time. Don't forget, we still have two days in which to come clean with my parents."

THIRTEEN

When Billie arrived home shortly after three o'clock that afternoon, she found her parents talking excitedly in hushed whispers at the kitchen table and writing down figures. They tried to hide the sheet of paper as she sat next to her mother.

"You two look as though you're plotting the overthrow of our government," Billie said teasingly. "What's up?"

Martha Foster hesitated. "Well, dear, you know that little house I told you about?" When Billie nodded, she went on. "Your father and I drove out to see it. Oh, Billie, it's cute as a button!"

"Where's Cord?" Billie asked, clenching and unclenching her fists nervously.

"He ran home for a change of clothes," Joe said. "I understand he still lives with his father. Isn't that odd for a man his age?"

"I think he moved back to be with his father

after his mother died last year," Billie said, thankful she wasn't a wooden puppet with a nose that grew every time she fibbed. "To sort of offer support." She couldn't very well tell her parents Cord's home was his family's ancestral mansion or that it was so large that Cord and his father could spend six months under its roof without bumping into each other. Her parents had received enough surprises in the past ten hours without having to bear the discomfort of a multimillionaire son-in-law. And Billie knew her parents, simple as they were, would be nervous. Her father would have to tell him how many credit cards he'd refused because he was a man who believed in paying cash for everything, and her mother would talk in that high-pitched voice she used when the minister dropped by unexpectedly.

"Such a nice boy," Martha said. It was obvious she was crazy about her daughter's new husband. "He didn't tell us much about his mother, only that she died in a car accident." She reached for the sheet of paper under her husband's elbow. "Now, look, Billie, about this house—"

"Don't you think we're rushing things a bit?" Billie asked, wishing Cord would get back so he could help fend them off.

"Let me talk to her, Martha." Joe Foster leaned forward on his elbows. "You know, your mother and I don't have a lot of money, Billie, but we still want to do things for you."

"Daddy, I don't expect—"

He waved her off. "I know you don't expect anything. That's what makes it so nice. We'd planned to give you a wedding. Nothing fancy, mind you, but something you could remember for the rest of your life." When Billie continued to glance nervously at the front door, her father got frustrated. "You talk to her, Martha. I've never been able to get her to listen."

"What your father is trying to say is that we've already made a down payment on this house," Martha said, her voice wavering with uncertainty.

Billie swallowed with difficulty. "You did what?" She looked at her father, wondering what could make a sensible, well-balanced man do something so uncharacteristically dumb. The answer was simple. Her mother had talked him into it. When Martha Foster got that certain look on her face, she could convince her husband to do the Achy-Breaky Heart Dance across a bed of hot coals.

"I know we probably rushed into it," her mother began, "but if you could see this place. And there was another couple interested in it, so we were afraid—"

"You bought me a house before I even had a chance to look at it?" Billie said in disbelief.

"We didn't actually buy it, we simply put a thousand dollars earnest money down. You'll like it, dear, I promise you. The man who owns it is going into a nursing home and is very motivated to sell. Your father even managed to get him down on his price."

Billie's head was spinning. To some people, a thousand dollars wasn't much. To her parents, it was more than they could truly afford. "I wish you hadn't done that," she said, shaking her head sadly.

"Before you say anything, come with us and look at it," her mother said. She got up and went for her pocketbook. Her husband pushed his chair out from the table as well.

Billie looked at them. "You mean now?"

"The realtor promised to meet us back out there at four o'clock. It's only a fifteen-minute drive."

Billie knew it was useless arguing. Nevertheless, she felt ten years old again, forced to eat peas and bring home *B*'s in math. Sighing heavily, she pushed her chair from the table and started for the door. She would look at the house if it meant that much to them. Not that she had any intention of buying anything that would tie her to Ruckers, mind you. She would look, but she knew she wouldn't like it.

A moment later she was following her parents down the stairs toward their older-model car when Cord pulled into the drive in his shiny Corvette. Joe Foster took a long, hard look at the car, and it was obvious he was trying to calculate what something like it would cost. He waited until Cord climbed out before saying anything.

"That must've set you back a pretty penny," he said, nodding toward the car.

Cord exchanged nervous glances with Billie. "What, this old thing?" he said, patting the hood. "Naw, I bought it used. After it had been wrecked. Hit a tree doing forty," he added, when he saw his first comments weren't going to fly. "You'd never know it had been junked for trash. Where's everybody going?" he asked, wanting to change the subject when even Martha seemed to have trouble believing the sleek machine had ever had so much as a dent in it.

Billie smiled at him in a way that suggested after what she was about to tell him, he might want to climb back in his automobile and look for a new tree to run into. "Mom and Dad went out and bought us a house this afternoon," she said. "Wasn't that nice of them?"

Try as he might, Cord couldn't think of an intelligent response. "No kidding?"

Martha stepped forward. "Cord, dear, I don't want you to think we're trying to run your life. It's just—" She paused. "Joe and I know how hard it is for newlyweds. And Billie has all those college loans to pay back. We wanted to help in any way we could."

"That's very generous of you," Cord said, knowing they probably couldn't afford to be. He looked to Billie for help in handling the situation, but the look on her face said, "Swim or sink, buster."

Joe walked over and slapped Cord on the back. "What do you say we all ride out and have a look at it, son? If you and Billie don't like it, I'll try to get my money back."

Cord knew exactly what it meant to be between a rock and a hard place. "Fine with me," he managed.

The house resembled a log cabin of sorts, tucked in the woods with a creek running behind it. While Billie's parents chatted briefly with the realtor, who was waiting to take them through, Cord took a moment to chat with Billie. "Can they really afford to do this?" he asked.

"No. But try telling them that."

"It's kinda cute, though, isn't it?" he said, tilting his head to the side as though studying it closely.

It was more than cute; it was downright adorable, and Billie loved it. Agreeing to see it had been a mistake. "What are we going to do with a house, Cord?" she said, directing her words at herself as well. "We . . . I mean, I already have a place to live. And I can't afford these payments no matter what a good deal it is." She shook her head as she recalled what she still owed for her education. "This is what happens when you lie. It keeps escalating until it's out of control." She was prevented from saying anything further when her parents motioned for them to follow.

The house was, as Martha had said earlier, cute as a button and fully furnished since the owner would not need furniture in the nursing home. Although it had only two bedrooms, the rooms were spacious, with plenty of windows to let in light. The kitchen would be wonderful with new paint and paper, Billie decided. The living room, or great room as the realtor called it, was paneled in tongue-and-groove with a massive fireplace on one wall, and cozy overstuffed furniture. While the house wouldn't have been big enough for a growing family, it was perfect for a young married couple and would easily accommodate a new baby if such was the case. Martha's words. A large Jacuzzi had been installed in the bathroom.

"The owner's wife had a bad back," the realtor said. "He had this installed several years ago before she died."

"What do you think?" Cord asked Billie when they ventured out back to look at the creek.

"It would be just right if I was in the market for a house," she told him. She knew now why her parents had been so excited about the place. It was indeed lovely with its rustic features and woodsy setting. "What are we going to do now?" she said, turning to Cord.

He shook his head. "I don't know. I'm so overwhelmed with what they did for us. I would have been happy with a blender or a vacuum cleaner."

Billie wanted to punch him for making jokes at a time like this. "You're no help," she muttered.

"What do you think, dear?" Martha Foster asked, coming up behind her daughter.

Billie whirled around, startled. "Oh, it's lovely, Mother. Really lovely."

"I love it," Cord said, giving the woman a smile that would have made his dentist proud. "But I'd love it even more if you and Mr. Foster would let me reimburse you the thousand dollars."

"Nonsense. It's our wedding gift to you. And from now on, you can call us Mom and Dad." She paused as her daughter continued to frown. "Are you sure you like it, Billie, dear? You have a funny look on your face."

"I love it, Mom," she said, going over to kiss her mother on the cheek. "I'm just overwhelmed at the moment," she said, falling back on the word Cord had used when her poor dazed mind refused to supply her with a fresh one.

"I don't want either of you to worry about getting a loan," Joe Foster said when he joined them in the backyard a few minutes later. "I've always had very good credit. So good, in fact, that I'm always having to return those credit cards they send me in the mail. I'll be glad to co-sign if you need me to."

Billie felt her cheeks burn, embarrassed for her father. Here he was, barely making ends meet, and he was offering to help a multimillionaire get a loan. Of course, there was no way for her parents to know Cord was rich. They had lied and deceived them every step of the way. Billie had never known such shame. The look on Cord's face told her he was feeling much the same.

"Daddy, that's very generous of you," she began, only to be interrupted by Cord.

"Thank you, sir," Cord said, sticking his hand out to shake with her father. "I'll talk to someone at the bank and get back with you if we need your help."

The realtor joined them, holding a clipboard. "So, how do the newlyweds like their new home?" she asked.

"They're crazy about it," Martha said, grinning so wide, Billie feared her upper plate would fall out. "By the way, I haven't introduced you to my daughter and her new husband." Nobody saw the tense look Billie and Cord exchanged. "This is my daughter, Billie," she began, then paused long enough to remind the realtor she was a doctor. "And this is her husband, Cord Buford."

"You're not Cordell Buford?" the realtor said, her surprise clearly evident. "Arthur Buford's son?"

"That's me," Cord said, realizing they might have painted themselves into yet another corner. The realtor was staring blatantly. It was obvious she was wondering why a Buford was looking to buy a modest cabin along a creek when he could afford a castle if he wanted.

"I hadn't realized you'd married," she said, still

wearing a perplexed frown. "I didn't see anything in the society column."

"They flew to Vegas for one of those quickie weddings," Martha said. "Of course, we've insisted they do it right, so they're to be married Wednesday night by a minister."

"Perhaps you'd like to see something a little larger," the woman said. "I mean, this cabin is cute enough, but you might want something nicer for entertaining."

"No, this is perfect," Cord assured her.

"We don't want them getting in over their heads," Joe said.

The realtor nodded as though it made complete sense. "Yes, well, I can understand that."

An uncomfortable silence ensued. Billie was the first to break it. "I don't know about the rest of you, but I'm starved. Why don't we go out to dinner?" She looked at Cord. "And we know just the place, don't we? It's a little out of the way, but the food is wonderful."

Cord picked up on her hint right away. She wanted to go someplace where he wouldn't be recognized. "Sounds good to me," he said. They thanked the realtor, who was still frowning, and made their way back to the car. Billie didn't draw a breath of relief until they hit the next town.

<hr>

The following morning Billie was awakened by the telephone ringing on her nightstand. Beside her, Cord stirred and pulled the covers to his chin. By unspoken agreement he was sticking to his side of the bed. Not only because Billie was a wreck with all that was happening, but because her parents were in the next room. That in itself was enough to dull anyone's sexual appetite, he'd decided.

Billie grabbed the phone on the second ring, thinking there must be an emergency at the clinic. "Dr. Foster," she said, waiting for the nasal-sounding woman who worked for the clinic's answering service to reply.

"This is Arthur Buford," the voice on the other end said instead. "Is my son there?"

Billie blinked, coming wide awake. "Uh, yes, Mr. Buford. Just one second, please." Holding her hand over the receiver, she shook Cord. "Wake up," she said, trying to keep her voice down so as not to wake her parents as well. "Your father's on the phone."

"My father?" Cord gazed back at her. "What the hell does he want?" He took the telephone from her, mumbled into it, then was quiet for a moment. Finally, he rubbed his eyes and spoke. "Can we discuss this later?" he asked, his voice taking on a cool tone. "Yeah, I'll be there in half an hour." He handed Billie the receiver.

Billie hung up the telephone. "What did he want?"

Cord fell back on the bed with a heavy sigh. "Two things, actually. First, he wanted to congratulate me on my upcoming marriage."

"What?"

"Our names were listed in the paper this morning as having applied for a marriage license yesterday afternoon."

"Oh, no!" She thought of Dr. Barnaby and Nurse Bradshaw and wondered what she was going to tell them. When had her life become so unmanageable? "What else did he want?"

Cord looked at her for a long, silent moment. "He wanted to let me know that someone has filed a complaint with the Labor Board, stating that Buford Textiles is unsafe."

Billie felt her heart plummet. "Are you serious?"

He stared at the ceiling. "Dead serious."

"What are you going to do?"

"Why do you ask?"

She didn't miss the anger in his voice. "Cord, you don't think I filed that complaint, do you?"

He gazed at her, then climbed out of bed and reached for his clothes. "I don't know what to think right now, if you want to know the truth. I'd planned to go in and investigate right away until—" He paused. "Until this other thing came up with your folks."

"Where are you going?"

"I have to meet with my father and Bill Crenshaw at the house. Our attorney is already there. Once the press gets wind of this—" He didn't finish his sentence.

"I didn't do it, Cord," she said, climbing out of the bed. "I wouldn't do such a thing without telling you first. You have to believe me."

He nodded, then dressed in silence. He slipped out the front door without another word.

Billie had showered and dressed by the time her parents woke up. Her father went downstairs for the paper while her mother sipped her first cup of coffee. She studied Billie from over the rim of her cup.

"Is something wrong, dear?" she asked. "You look worried this morning."

"I'm fine," Billie told her. "I guess I have a lot on my mind."

"Well, you've been through a lot these past few days, what with getting married and all." Martha Foster patted her hand. "I can't help but feel guilty now for making your life more stressful over this house business. Your father and I talked about it last night and decided if you and Cord don't want it, we'll forfeit our earnest money. It would serve us right for interfering the way we did."

Billie was almost moved to tears by her mother's words. She laid her head on her mother's hand. "Mom, I know you did it because you love me, but—" She paused and sniffed. "I wish you and Dad would have used the money for yourselves. You've given me enough already."

"It makes us feel good to help," Martha said, her own eyes growing misty as she patted her daughter's head. "Especially your father."

Billie raised up and wiped her eyes. "What do you mean?"

"He felt so guilty after your brother died. He thought maybe if we'd had more money and could afford to take him to specialists, he would have lived longer."

"What kind of life would it have been?" Billie said gently. "He was not able to do the things he loved anymore. I think Byron would have preferred death to living the kind of life he was forced to live in the end."

Martha nodded. "He pretty much said the same thing to me during those last days," she said, her voice taking on a tender note. She blinked back fresh tears and hurried to the coffeemaker as Joe came into the apartment, wished them good morning, then turned on the portable television set in the living room. He switched it to the news and took a seat in a nearby chair.

Billie watched her mother carry the coffee to her father and kiss him lightly on the lips. He smiled and patted her behind, then sipped his coffee in silence as he watched the morning news. She had seen her parents at their worst, burying a son who was too young to die, trying to pay doctors' bills and funeral expenses. Yet they seldom had a cross word for each other. Adversity had not torn them apart as it did so many couples. If anything, it had made their love stronger. Billie knew, in her heart, that was why she had stayed single all these years. She wanted a man who, after thirty years of marriage, looked at her the way her father looked at her mother. Her mind automatically pulled up a picture of Cord. Was it possible that the worst rogue of them all could be tamed by love?

"So, what would you two like to do today?" Billie asked, trying to put all the sentimental stuff aside before she became weepy again. Was this what falling in love did to a person? She waited for them to answer, then saw that her parents were focused on the TV screen.

"Isn't that Cord?" her mother asked.

Billie snapped her head around as her father hurried to the television set and turned up the volume. Sure enough, it was Cord, walking beside his father through the front doors of Buford Textiles. A newsman asked Arthur Buford about the investigation going on inside the mill by OSHA officials, but the man had no comment to make at that time, he told them. Both Cord and his father disappeared inside, leaving Bill Crenshaw behind to smooth things over.

"Mr. Crenshaw, you're the plant manager here, is that right?" the newsman asked.

"That is correct," he said, giving the camera a

warm smile. If Cord and his father had looked nervous about the situation, Bill Crenshaw looked anything but.

"Could you tell us what's going on in the mill this morning?" the other man asked.

"It's simple," Crenshaw said. "Buford Textiles is being investigated for claims of unsafe working conditions."

"*Buford* Textiles?" Joe said, glancing at Billie.

"Shhh, Daddy!" She hushed him so she could listen.

"And do you know who filed the report?" the newsman asked.

"Not at this time."

"Do you believe Buford Textiles is unsafe, Mr. Crenshaw?"

"Certainly not. Our mills have been setting safety standards for years now. We feel this investigation will only prove that claim."

"Yes, but isn't it true that the senior Mr. Buford has tried to keep these work-related illnesses hush-hush until now?"

"He was merely trying to prevent people from panicking."

"You're close friends with Arthur Buford, aren't you, sir?"

"Very close."

"Rumor has it that he's a cold man to work for. Is that true?"

Bill Crenshaw had wearied of the questions. "That's all the time I have for now," he said, starting inside the door.

"Isn't it true that Mr. Buford's wife was killed in an auto accident last year in an attempt to leave him?"

All the color drained out of Crenshaw's face, and his eyes took on a wild, savage look that startled Billie as she watched. He grabbed the newsman by the collar. "I'd thank you not to drag her into this, you piece of—" The picture went blank.

"What in the world?" Martha said, turning to look at Billie.

When the picture returned, the newsman was standing before the camera looking slightly shaken. His tie was loose, his hair mussed, but he was doing everything in his power to remain professional. He mumbled something about returning once they had more information on the investigation going on at Buford Textiles, then signed off.

Joe Foster stood and regarded his daughter with a look that would have melted steel. "What the hell is going on here?" he demanded.

Billie, stunned by what she'd seen on TV, didn't answer right away. Finally, she faced them, feeling sixteen again. "Mom, Dad, I think it's time we talked."

FOURTEEN

Billie did not hear from Cord for the rest of the day. She tried to call him at the mill twice, but his secretary said he was in a meeting and could not be disturbed.

Dinnertime came, and nobody seemed hungry, despite the fact that Martha had made Billie's favorite, stuffed Cornish hens. They were in the process of cleaning up when Cord knocked on the door.

Billie was so surprised to see him, she didn't know what to say. His eyes were slightly puffy and red, and she asked him if he was getting a cold. He shrugged; then they all stood there for a moment feeling uncomfortable. As if sensing the two needed to be alone, Martha suggested she and Joe take a walk.

"Your mother looks as if she's been crying," Cord said.

"She has. On and off since this morning." When he looked confused, she went on. "I told them the truth, Cord."

"Oh, damn." He sighed and raked his hands through his hair. "How'd they take it?"

"Well enough, I suppose. I told them I'd pay them back the thousand dollars they put on the house."

"I'll pay them back," he said. "After all, I'm the one who started this mess."

"It's not all your fault. Once they got over their hurt, we had a long talk. You were right. My parents and I have been carrying around some leftover guilt due to my brother's death. I don't want to do anything to hurt them, and they want to protect me. I guess we've got to get over that." She paused and folded her arms in front of her, and for a moment she was near tears again. "Anyway, they're leaving first thing in the morning. I would appreciate it if you'd"—she paused and swallowed—"cancel with the minister."

All the light went out of his eyes. She wasn't willing to take a chance on him. She said she loved him, and he knew he loved her, but that wasn't enough. He nodded after a moment. "Yeah, okay." He shifted his feet, wanting to say more, feeling there was so much more to say. She wanted guarantees because she had suffered enough hurt in her life, but there were no guarantees in life and no telling where their future would lead them. The only sure thing he could offer was his love, and that wasn't enough. "Well, I'd better go," he said. "I need to get back to the mill."

"Have they found anything?"

"Nothing." He met her gaze. "I know you didn't file the complaint, Billie. Kay Nettles did it. She got scared, worrying about what might happen to her grandchildren if her condition got worse. I don't blame her. Anyway, I'm sorry for doubting you."

"That's okay." She followed him to the door, wishing he would at least put his arms around her before he left. "You want something for your eyes before you go?" she asked, trying to sound casual despite the fact that her heart was breaking. The past two days had been unusual, but she had never been happier than in the moments she'd spent with him. "They look awful."

He rubbed them. "I've already put something in them, but it doesn't help. I must be getting a cold. I've been hacking all day."

"Cord?" He paused at the door. "You're helping with the investigation, right?" He nodded. "Be sure to wear something over your mouth while you're in there. It's probably just a cold like you say, but I don't want you taking chances."

He nodded and made his way out the door.

❖———————❖

Billie tossed and turned in her bed for two hours, but she couldn't get to sleep no matter how she tried. Something was bothering her. Well, *a lot* was bothering her, but there was something she couldn't quite put her finger on. It was shortly after 2:00 A.M. when she called Cord at home. Lula answered the phone in a sleepy voice.

"This is Billie Foster, Lula," she said. "I need to talk to Cord."

Cord picked up on an extension a minute later. "Billie, what's wrong?"

"I need to talk to you about something," she said. "Can you meet me at the mill?"

"Now?"

"It's very important, Cord."

"Yeah, okay."

Billie slipped out of the apartment a few minutes later dressed in jeans and a T-shirt. She left a note for her parents in case they woke, telling them she had an emergency. Well, it wasn't altogether untrue, she told herself as she made her way to her car.

She arrived at the mill twenty minutes later and parked near the entrance where Cord was already waiting. She climbed out as he hurried over. "What's going on?" he asked.

"Your eyes are still a bit puffy," she told him. "How do they feel?"

"Better. Why?"

"Can you get me into the weave room?"

He hesitated. "I'm not sure. There's a guard at the door. The room has been sealed off pending the investigation."

"Then we'll ask the guard," she said matter-of-factly.

Minutes later they found themselves in the weave room with the guard beside them. "Remember, you can look, but you can't touch anything," he warned.

"What are you looking for?" Cord asked Billie.

"I'm not sure."

He rubbed his tired eyes. "You woke me up at this hour, and you're not sure why we're here?"

"Cord, I don't know the first thing about heating and air, but would it be possible to vent carbon monoxide through an air vent into this room?"

He shook his head. "This part of the mill isn't air-conditioned. That's why we have these big fans. You would only be able to vent carbon monoxide in from the furnace, and we don't run the furnace this time of year. Besides, if the employees were suffering from carbon-monoxide poisoning, we would know it."

"How would you know? It's colorless and odorless."

"Yeah, but there are sure signs, Billie."

"Right. Nausea, dizziness, and headaches. Look, I'm not saying it's carbon monoxide, but what if some sort of chemical or gas was being vented into this room?" When he looked doubtful, she went on.

"Normal blood tests don't measure the acidity or the amount of oxygen and carbon monoxide, Cord. That takes an entirely different type of test. The blood must be drawn directly from an artery. That could very well be the reason all the blood tests I did on the weavers were negative." She stiffened at the look he gave her. "You don't believe me. You think I'm making excuses as to why nothing showed up in those blood tests."

"That's not it at all," he said, "I'm merely trying to deal with the fact that you believe it's an act of sabotage. Anyway, whatever it is, it's not coming in through the vents. That's the first thing we checked. The vents aren't even being used this time of year."

"Okay, tell me about those little gadgets that shoot moisture into the air," she said, pointing toward the pipe running along the ceiling. "You know, those jets that are supposed to keep the dust levels down."

Something flickered in his black eyes as he pondered the possibilities. Cord looked at the guard. "Could we get a closer look at those jets?"

"Not without an inspector present."

"Would you mind calling one?"

The guard looked surprised. "Now?"

"Now."

Arthur Buford looked dead on his feet when he entered the mill shortly after sunup. He found Billie and Cord sipping coffee and talking to one of the OSHA inspectors. "Is it true?" he asked his son. "Someone inside has been trying to poison our employees?"

"We don't know anything for certain," the inspector said. "We've removed the jets and are transporting them to a lab right now. All I can tell you at this time is that the mist coming from them is definitely not simple water."

"Oh, Lord," Arthur said, the color draining from his face. "Who would do such a thing?"

The inspector seemed to ponder it. "Mr. Buford, are there any employees in the mill who are unhappy with their working conditions? I understand you're not unionized."

Cord saw that his father was too distressed to speak. "Our workers voted against becoming union," he said. "Mainly because we *do* offer safe working conditions and fair wages."

"Whoever did this is smart," Billie said. "Not only did this person know how to get the chemical in here without notice, he or she was also smart enough to use something that wouldn't show up in a normal examination."

"You'd need a damn engineer and chemist to figure that out," Arthur Buford said.

"Who do you know would fit those qualifications?"

"Nobody that I know of."

Billie thought she knew, but she waited until the safety inspector left them before she said anything. "May I ask you something very personal, Mr. Buford?" she said to the older man. When he nodded, she went on. "I know this is going to be painful, but I'd like the truth."

"What is it, Dr. Foster?" he said.

"When your wife was killed last year, she was leaving you, wasn't she?"

Cord looked surprised. His father's face became hard. "I don't see what that has to do with this, but yes, it's true she was leaving me. Any more embarrassing questions, Doctor?"

"Just one. Was she leaving you for another man?"

"Yes."

This time Cord's face took on a look of shock and outright horror. "You never told me that," he said, his voice holding an accusing tone.

"Why should I have?" the older man asked. "So you could think badly of her? She was dead." He looked at his son for a long moment. "Besides, we both know it was nothing less than I deserved. She only stayed with me out of necessity. Finally, she couldn't take it anymore." He turned to Billie. "Yes, my wife left me for another man. She was kind enough to leave a note saying as much."

"Do you have any idea who that man could have been?"

"No."

"Could that man have been Bill Crenshaw?"

It was shortly after eleven o'clock in the morning when Billie and Cord left the hospital, having taken arterial samples from the weavers to be analyzed. The fact that the employees had begun to feel better once removed from the weave room was enough to convince Billie they weren't dealing with anything serious or long-lasting. They drove straight to the clinic, where they discussed the situation at length with Dr. Barnaby, who promised to follow up.

"I suppose you'll be expecting an apology," he told Billie, once Cord had excused himself to make a phone call.

"Not unless you have a gun I can put to your head," she said.

He chuckled. "You think I'm too old to practice, don't you?"

She shook her head. "No, I think you have a few good years left yet."

He stood and hitched his pants up to his belly. He gazed out the window at a beautiful summer day. "I don't know a whole lot about these modern treatments you young doctors are so good at. In my day we had to use what was available. We didn't have all these fancy wonder drugs they have today."

"There's a lot to be said for old-fashioned remedies, Dr. Barnaby," she said. She stood and walked over to him and looked out the window as well. "I'm going to tell you something if you promise not to gloat."

He looked at her for a moment. "What?"

"I would never have figured out what was happening to those weavers if it hadn't been for you."

He looked surprised. "How do you figure?"

"Remember Cara Miller and her poison ivy?" He nodded. "Well, I kept thinking that the mill workers were eating or touching something that was making them sick. It wasn't that at all. The chemical was getting into the pores of their skin and through eye tissue. I wouldn't have figured it out if Cord hadn't come by my place last night with puffy eyes. It made me think of Mrs. Miller and how bad her eyes had looked that day. Evidently, the eye problems disappeared after the workers left the mill, because I didn't notice puffiness on the other patients."

"Well, I'll be danged." He paused and reached behind his desk. "Speaking of Cord Buford," he said, pulling out a small box. "Nurse Bradshaw and I picked up something for the two of you. Your wedding present."

Billie's face turned red as she took the box he offered her. "Oh, Dr. Barnaby, I wish you hadn't."

"I don't know why the two of you were keeping it a secret. Everybody in this town knows you're crazy about each other."

Billie glanced around when she heard Cord come

up behind her. "Look," she said, giving him a fake smile. "Dr. Barnaby has given us a wedding present."

"You don't say." It was obvious Cord didn't know what to say.

"I'll update you on the mill workers once I take another look at them," the old doctor said. "And I'll be glad to share what we know with officials from your Asheville plant. I feel confident the effects shouldn't last more than a few days. Whoever did this obviously wasn't trying to kill anybody."

"No, I think whoever did it was trying to embarrass the Bufords," Billie said, then excused herself and Cord. "I need to drop by my office just a second," she said. They stepped into her modest office.

Cord closed the door behind them. "I want to talk to you," he said. "Alone."

Billie had already picked up the phone to call her parents, who'd decided to put off their trip until late afternoon so they could catch up on what was happening at the mill. She put the phone down. "What is it?"

"Bill Crenshaw was picked up an hour ago by the police. They got a full confession. It won't surprise you to know he's responsible for the Asheville plant as well. And that's not all. They found a small laboratory set up in his basement. It was sort of a hobby with him."

"He also worked in the lab at the mill for a while, from what I understand."

"He claims he wasn't trying to kill anybody, and the chemical will wear off completely in a matter of weeks. What made you suspect him?"

"He'd worked in all the departments before becoming manager. He also told me he was the one who introduced your parents. You told me they were engaged once and that you believed your mother regretted marrying your father from the beginning. I believe your mother was leaving your father that night to run off with Bill. She died in that attempt. I don't think Bill ever got over it, and he blamed your father for not showing her the happiness she deserved, for caring more for his mills than for his own wife."

"So one way to get back at my old man is to embarrass him."

"It worked. Your dad looked like death warmed over this morning." She paused. "I think he has suffered enough over this, Cord. So have you."

Cord pondered her words for a long moment. "Yeah, I know you're right. I guess it's time we bury this hatchet between us." He looked at her. "But first, you and I have some unfinished business."

"What do you mean?"

"About the minister. I forgot to cancel."

"Cord!" She rose from her seat.

He rounded the desk. "No, that's a lie," he said. "I didn't forget to cancel. I didn't want to. I was getting used to the idea of being married to you and spending some time alone in that cabin by the creek." When she continued to look shocked, he went on. "Listen to me, dammit," he said, raising his voice slightly. "I don't care *where* we live. You want to leave this town after you're finished here, then I'll go with you. I can live anywhere as long as I'm near an airport. But that's not what's important, and you know it. What's important is that I love you and you love me." He paused when she continued to stare back at him in silence. "I even managed to find time to run by a jewelry store," he said, pulling a small velvet box from his pocket. He opened it to reveal two wedding bands. "What d'you say, Doc? If you turn me down, you know it's going to break my heart, and there's not a darn thing you can do to mend one of those."

He looked so handsome and sincere that Billie had trouble believing he was hers. "Come here, you big rogue," she said, laughter bubbling up from her throat. He grinned and went to her, setting the box on her desk for the time being. They embraced. Finally, he kissed her hard on the lips.

"Does this mean yes?" he asked eagerly.

"I'm still thinking about it," she said, a smile teasing the corners of her lips. "Do you promise to be faithful to me, Cord Buford?" she said. " 'Cause if you don't, I'll take my scalpel to you and cut your liver out and serve it to you on a plate."

"I love this docile side of you, Doc." He kissed her again. "What makes you think I'd ever want to stray? Do you think I don't know a good thing when I see it?" He shook his head. "I'm crazy mad in love with you, Billie Foster, and I know you feel the same, don't you?"

"Yes, Cord," she said, her eyes shining with love for the man. "I love you so much, it hurts." She loved him so much that nothing seemed to matter, least of all where they lived. But it was nice to know he was willing to leave if she wanted. That knowledge would make it easier for her to stay.

His own eyes grew tender. "Marry me, baby. I promise you won't regret it. We can spend a year or so in that cabin, then maybe let your parents have it when your dad retires. You know I won't ever let your family want for anything."

She was touched to the core. Billie managed to free one of her hands. She picked up the phone, anchored it between her shoulder and ear, and dialed. "Mom, it's me," she said. "Yes, I'll be home in a few minutes, and I'll tell you everything. Oh, and Mom—" She paused and smiled. "Ask Daddy if the two of you can hang around a little longer. Cord and I have decided to make that wedding tonight after all." Billie held the phone away from her ear as her mother squealed with happiness, then yelled for her husband. Billie gently placed the receiver in its cradle. "Now, all you have to do is call and invite your father," she said.

Cord pulled her roughly against him. "There's plenty of time for that, but right now, I very much want to kiss my bride-to-be."

THE EDITOR'S CORNER

There's never too much of a good thing when it comes to romances inspired by beloved stories, so next month we present TREASURED TALES II. Coming your way are six brand-new LOVESWEPTs written by some of the most talented authors of romantic fiction today. You'll delight in their contemporary versions of age-old classics . . . and experience the excitement and passion of falling in love. TREASURED TALES II— what a way to begin the new year!

The first book in our fabulous line up is **PERFECT DOUBLE** by Cindy Gerard, LOVESWEPT #660. In this wonderful retelling of *The Prince and the Pauper* business mogul Logan Prince gets saved by a stranger from a near-fatal mugging, then wakes up in an unfamiliar bed to find a reluctant angel with a siren's body bandaging his wounds! Logan vows to win Carmen Sanchez's heart—

even if it means making a daring bargain with his look-alike rescuer and trading places with the cowboy drifter. It take plenty of wooing before Carmen surrenders to desire—and even more sweet persuasion to regain her trust once he confesses to his charade. A top-notch story from talented Cindy.

Homer's epic poem *The Odyssey* has never been as romantic as Billie Green's version, **BABY, COME BACK**, LOVESWEPT #661. Like Odysseus, David Moore has spent a long time away from home. Finally free after six years in captivity, and with an unrecognizable face and voice, he's not sure if there's still room for him in the lives of his sweet wife, Kathy, and their son, Ben. When he returns home, he masquerades as a handyman, determined to be close to his son, aching to show his wife that, though she's now a successful businesswoman, she still needs him. Poignant and passionate, this love story shows Billie at her finest!

Tom Falconson lives the nightmare of *The Invisible Man* in Terry Lawrence's **THE SHADOW LOVER**, LOVESWEPT #662. When a government experiment goes awry and renders the dashingly virile intelligence agent invisible, Tom knows he has only one person to turn to. Delighted by mysteries, ever in search of the unexplained, Alice Willow opens her door to him, offering him refuge and the sensual freedom to pull her dangerously close. But even as Tom sets out to show her that the phantom in her arms is a flesh-and-blood man, he wonders if their love is strong enough to prove that nothing is impossible. Terry provides plenty of thrills and tempestuous emotions in this fabulous tale.

In Jan Hudson's **FLY WITH ME**, LOVESWEPT #663, Sawyer Hayes is a modern-day Peter Pan who soars through the air in a gleaming helicopter. He touches down in Pip LeBaron's backyard with an offer of a job in his company, but the computer genius quickly informs him that for now she's doing nothing except making up for the childhood she missed. Bewitched by her delicate beauty, Sawyer decides to help her, though her kissable mouth persuades him that a few grown-up games would be more fun. Pip soon welcomes his tantalizing embrace, turning to liquid moonlight beneath his touch. But is there a future together for a man who seems to live for fun and a lady whose work has been her whole life? Jan weaves her magic in this enchanting romance.

"The Ugly Duckling" was Linda Cajio's inspiration for her new LOVESWEPT, **HE'S SO SHY**, #664—and if there ever was an ugly duckling, Richard Creighton was it. Once a skinny nerd with glasses, he's now impossibly sexy, irresistibly gorgeous, and the hottest actor on the big screen. Penelope Marsh can't believe that this leading man in her cousin's movie is the same person she went to grade school with. She thinks he's definitely out of her league, but Richard doesn't agree. Drawn to the willowy schoolteacher, Richard dares her to accept what's written in the stars—that she's destined to be his leading lady for life. Linda delivers a surefire hit.

Last, but certainly not least, is **ANIMAL MAGNETISM** by Bonnie Pega, LOVESWEPT #665. Only Dr. Dolittle is Sebastian Kent's equal when it comes to relating to animals—but Danni Sullivan insists the veterinarian still needs her help. After all, he's new in her hometown, and no one knows every cat, bull, and pig there as well as she. For once giving in to impulse, Sebastian hires her on the spot—then thinks twice about it when her touch arouses long-denied yearnings. He can charm any beast, but he definitely needs a lesson in how to soothe his wounded heart. And Danni has just the right touch to heal his pain—and make him believe in love once more. Bonnie will delight you with this thoroughly enchanting story.

Happy reading!

With warmest wishes,

Nita Taublib

Nita Taublib

Associate Publisher

P.S. Don't miss the fabulous women's fiction Bantam has coming in January: **DESIRE**, the newest novel from bestselling author Amanda Quick; **LONG TIME COMING,** Sandra Brown's classic contemporary romance; **STRANGER IN MY ARMS** by R. J. Kaiser, a novel of romantic suspense in which a woman who has lost her memory is in danger of also losing her life; and **WHERE DOLPHINS GO** by LOVESWEPT author Peggy Webb, a truly unique romance that integrates into its story the fascinating ability of dolphins to aid injured children. We'll be giving you a sneak peek at these wonderful books in next month's LOVESWEPTs. And immediately following this page, look for a preview of the exciting women's novels from Bantam that are *available now!*

Don't miss these exciting books by your favorite Bantam authors

On sale in November:

ADAM'S FALL
by *Sandra Brown*

NOTORIOUS
by *Patricia Potter*

PRINCESS OF THIEVES
by *Katherine O'Neal*

CAPTURE THE NIGHT
by *Geralyn Dawson*

And in hardcover from Doubleday
ON WINGS OF MAGIC
by *Kay Hooper*

Adam's Fall

Available this month in hardcover
from *New York Times*
bestselling author

SANDRA BROWN

Over the past few years, Lilah Mason had watched her sister Elizabeth find love, get married, and have children, while she's been more than content to channel her energies into a career. A physical therapist with an unsinkable spirit and unwavering compassion, she's one of the best in the field. But when Lilah takes on a demanding new case, her patient's life isn't the only one transformed. She's never had a tougher patient than Adam, who challenges her methods and authority at every turn. Yet Lilah is determined to help him recover the life he's lost. What she can't see is that while she's winning Adam's battle, she's losing her heart. Now, as professional duty and passionate yearnings clash, Lilah must choose the right course for them both.

Sizzling Romance from One of the
World's Hottest Pens

Winner of *Romantic Times*'s
1992 Storyteller of the Year Award

Patricia Potter

Nationally bestselling author of
Renegade and **Lightning**

NOTORIOUS

*The owner of the most popular saloon in San Francisco,
Catalina Hilliard knows Marsh Canton is trouble the
moment she first sees him. He's not the first to attempt to
open a rival saloon next door to the Silver Slipper, but he
does possess a steely strength that was missing from the
men she'd driven out of business. Even more perilous to
Cat's plans is the spark of desire that flares between
them, a desire that's about to spin her carefully orchestrated life out of control . . .*

"We have nothing to discuss," she said coldly,
even as she struggled to keep from trembling. All
her thoughts were in disarray. He was so adept at
personal invasion. That look in his eyes of pure radi-
ance, of physical need, almost burned through her.

Fifteen years. Nearly fifteen years since a man
had touched her so intimately. And he was doing
it only with his eyes!

And, dear Lucifer, she was responding.

She'd thought herself immune from desire. If
she'd ever had any, she believed it had been killed

long ago by brutality and shame and utter abhorrence of an act that gave men power and left her little more than a thing to be used and hurt. She'd never felt this bubbling, boiling warmth inside, this craving that was more than physical hunger.

That's what frightened her most of all.

But she wouldn't show it. She would never show it! She didn't even like Canton, devil take him. She didn't like anything about him. And she would send him back to wherever he came. Tail between his legs. No matter what it took. And she would never feel desire again.

But now she had little choice, unless she wished to stand here all afternoon, his hand burning a brand into her. He wasn't going to let her go, and perhaps it was time to lay her cards on the table. She preferred open warfare to guerrilla fighting. She hadn't felt right about the kidnapping and beating—even if she did frequently regret her moment of mercy on his behalf.

She shrugged and his hand relaxed slightly. They left, and he flagged down a carriage for hire. Using those strangely elegant manners that still puzzled her, he helped her inside with a grace that would put royalty to shame.

He left her then for a moment and spoke to the driver, passing a few bills up to him, then returned and vaulted to the seat next to her. Hard-muscled thigh pushed against her leg; his tanned arm, made visible by the rolled-up sleeve, touched her much smaller one, the wiry male hair brushing against her skin, sparking a thousand tiny charges. His scent, a spicy mixture of bay and soap, teased her senses. Everything about him—the strength and power and raw masculinity that he made no attempt to conceal—made her feel fragile, delicate.

But not vulnerable, she told herself. Never vulnerable again. She would fight back by seizing control and keeping it.

She straightened her back and smiled. A seductive smile. A smile that had entranced men for the last ten years. A practiced smile that knew exactly how far to go. A kind of promise that left doors opened, while permitting retreat. It was a smile that kept men coming to the Silver Slipper even as they understood they had no real chance of realizing the dream.

Canton raised an eyebrow. "You *are* very good," he said admiringly.

She shrugged. "It usually works."

"I imagine it does," he said. "Although I doubt if most of the men you use it on have seen the thornier part of you."

"Most don't irritate me as you do."

"Irritate, Miss Cat?"

"Don't call me Cat. My name is Catalina."

"Is it?"

"Is yours really Taylor Canton?"

The last two questions were spoken softly, dangerously, both trying to probe weaknesses, and both recognizing the tactic of the other.

"I would swear to it on a Bible," Marsh said, his mouth quirking.

"I'm surprised you have one, or know what one is."

"I had a very good upbringing, Miss Cat." He emphasized the last word.

"And then what happened?" she asked caustically.

The sardonic amusement in his eyes faded. "A great deal. And what is your story?"

Dear God, his voice was mesmerizing, an intimate song that said nothing but wanted everything. Low and deep and provocative. Compelling. And irresistible . . . almost.

"I had a very poor upbringing," she said. "And then a great deal happened."

For the first time since she'd met him, she saw real humor in his eyes. Not just that cynical amusement as if he were some higher being looking down on a world inhabited by silly children. "You're the first woman I've met with fewer scruples than my own," he said, admiration again in his voice.

She opened her eyes wide. "You have some?"

"As I told you that first night, I don't usually mistreat women."

"Usually?"

"Unless provoked."

"A threat, Mr. Canton?"

"I never threaten, Miss Cat. Neither do I turn down challenges."

"And you usually win?"

"Not usually, Miss Cat. Always." The word was flat. Almost ugly in its surety.

"So do I," she said complacently.

Their voices, Cat knew, had lowered into little more than husky whispers. The air in the closed carriage was sparking, hissing, crackling. Threatening to ignite. His hand moved to her arm, his fingers running up and down it in slow, caressingly sensuous trails.

And then the heat surrounding them was as intense as that in the heart of a volcano. Intense and violent. She wondered very briefly if this was a version of hell. She had just decided it was when he bent toward her, his lips brushing over hers.

And heaven and hell collided.

PRINCESS OF THIEVES
by
Katherine O'Neal

"A brilliant new talent bound to
make her mark on the genre."
—Iris Johansen

*Mace Blackwood is the greatest con artist in the world,
a demon whose family is responsible for the death of
Saranda Sherwin's parents. And though he might be
luring her to damnation itself, Saranda allows herself to be set aflame by the fire in his dark eyes. It's a
calculated surrender that he finds both intoxicating
and infuriating, for one evening alone with the
blue-eyed siren can never be enough. And now he
will stop at nothing to have her forever....*

Saranda could read his intentions in the gleam
of his midnight eyes. "Stay away from me," she
gasped.

"Surely, you're not afraid of me? I've already
admitted defeat."

"As if I'd trust anything you'd say."

Mace raised a brow. "Trust? No, sweetheart, it's
not about trust between us."

"You're right. It's about a battle between our
families that has finally come to an end. The

Sherwins have won, Blackwood. You have no further hand to play."

Even as she said it, she knew it wasn't true. Despite the bad blood between them, they had unfinished business. Because the game, this time, had gone too far.

"That's separate. The feud, the competition—that has nothing to do with what's happening between you and me."

"You must think I'm the rankest kind of amateur. Do you think I don't know what you're up to?"

He put his hand to her cheek and stroked the softly shadowed contours of her face. "What am I up to?"

He was so close, she could feel the muscles of his chest toying with her breasts. Against all sense, she hungered to be touched.

"If you can succeed in seducing me, you can run to Winston with the news—"

His hand drifted from her cheek down the naked column of her neck, to softly caress the slope of her naked shoulder. "I could tell him you slept with me whether you do or not. But you know as well as I do he wouldn't believe me."

"That argument won't work either, Blackwood," she said in a dangerously breathy tone.

"Very well, Miss Sherwin. Why don't we just lay our cards on the table?"

"Why not indeed?"

"Then here it is. I don't like you any more than you like me. In fact, I can't think of a woman I'd be less likely to covet. My family cared for yours no more than yours cared for mine. But I find myself in the unfortunate circumstance of wanting you to distraction. For some reason I can't even fathom, I can't look at you without wondering what you'd look like panting in my arms. Without wanting to feel your naked skin beneath my hands. Or taste your sweat on my tongue. Without needing to come inside you and make you cry out in passion and lose some of that *goddamned* control." A faint moan escaped her throat. "You're all I think about. You're like a fever in my brain. I keep thinking if I took you *just once*, I might finally expel you from my mind. So I don't suppose either of us is leaving this office before we've had what you came for."

"I came to tell you—"

"You could have done that any time. You could have left me wondering for the rest of the night if the wedding would take place. But you didn't wait. You knew if this was going to happen, it had to be tonight. Because once you're Winston's wife, I won't come near you. The minute you say 'I do,' you and I take off the gloves, darling, and the real battle begins. So it's now or never." He lowered his mouth to her shoulder, and her breath left her in a sigh.

"Now or never," she repeated in a daze.

"One night to forget who we are and what it all means. You're so confident of winning. Surely, you wouldn't deny me the spoils of the game. Or more to the point . . . deny yourself."

She looked up and met his sweltering gaze. After three days of not seeing him, she'd forgotten how devastatingly handsome he was. "I shan't fall in love with you, if that's what you're thinking. This will give you no advantage over me. I'm still going after you with both barrels loaded."

"Stop trying so hard to figure it out. I don't give a hang what you think of me. And I don't need your tender mercy. I tell you point-blank, if you think you've won, you may be in for a surprise. But that's beside the point." He wrapped a curl around his finger. Then, taking the pins from her hair, one by one, he dropped them to the floor. She felt her taut nerves jump as each pin clicked against the tile.

He ran both hands through the silvery hair, fluffing it with his fingers, dragging them slowly through the length as he watched the play of light on the silky strands. It spilled like moonlight over her shoulders. "Did you have to be so beautiful?" he rasped.

"Do you have to look so much like a Blackwood?"

He looked at her for a moment, his eyes piercing hers, his hands tangled in her hair. "Tell me what you want."

She couldn't look at him. It brought back memories of his brother she'd rather not relive. As it was, she couldn't believe she was doing this. But she had to have him. It was as elemental as food for her body and air to breathe. Her eyes dropped to his mouth—that blatant, sexual mouth that could make her wild with a grin or wet with a word.

She closed her eyes. If she didn't look at him, maybe she could separate this moment from the past. From what his brother had done. Her voice was a mere whisper when she spoke. "I want you to stop wasting time," she told him, "and make love to me."

He let go of her hair and took her naked shoulders in his hands. Bending her backward, he brought his mouth to hers with a kiss so searing, it scalded her heart.

CAPTURE THE NIGHT

by Geralyn Dawson

Award-winning author of

The Texan's Bride

"My highest praise goes to this author and her work, one of the best . . . I have read in years."
—*Rendezvous*

A desperate French beauty, the ruggedly handsome Texan who rescues her, and their precious stolen "Rose" are swept together by destiny as they each try to escape the secrets of their past.

Madeline groaned as the man called Sinclair sauntered toward her. This is all I need, she thought.

He stopped beside her and dipped into a perfect imitation of a gentleman's bow. Eyes shining, he looked up and said in his deplorable French, "Madame, do you by chance speak English? Apparently, we'll be sharing a spot in line. I beg to make your acquaintance."

She didn't answer.

He sighed and straightened. Then a wicked grin creased his face and in English he drawled, "Brazos Sinclair's my name, Texas born and bred. Most of my friends call me Sin, especially my lady friends. Nobody calls me Claire but once. I'll be sailin' with you on the *Uriel*."

Madeline ignored him.

Evidently, that bothered him not at all. "Cute baby," he said, peeking past the blanket. "Best keep him covered good though. This weather'll chill him."

Madeline bristled at the implied criticism. She glared at the man named Sin.

His grin faded. "Sure you don't speak English?"

She held her silence.

"Guess not, huh. That's all right, I'll enjoy conversin' with you anyway." He shot a piercing glare toward Victor Considérant, the colonists' leader and the man who had refused him a place on the *Uriel*. "I need a diversion, you see. Otherwise I'm liable to do something I shouldn't." Angling his head, he gave her another sweeping gaze. "You're a right fine lookin' woman, ma'am, a real beauty. Don't know that I think much of your husband, though, leavin' you here on the docks by your lonesome."

He paused and looked around, his stare snagging on a pair of scruffy sailors. "It's a dangerous thing for women to be alone in such a place, and for a beautiful one like you, well, I hesitate to think."

Obviously, Madeline said to herself.

The Texan continued, glancing around at the people milling along the wharf. " 'Course, I can't say I understand you Europeans. I've been here goin' on two years, and I'm no closer to figurin' y'all out now than I was the day I rolled off the boat." He reached into his jacket pocket and pulled out a pair of peppermint sticks.

Madeline declined the offer by shaking her head, and he returned one to his pocket before taking a slow lick of the second. "One thing, there's all those kings and royals. I think it's nothin' short of silly to climb on a high horse simply because blood family's been plowin' the same dirt for hundreds of years. I tell you what, ma'am, Texans aren't built for bowin'. It's been bred right out of us."

Brazos leveled a hard stare on Victor Considérant and shook his peppermint in the Frenchman's direction. "And aristocrats are just as bad as royalty. That fellow's one of the worst. Although I'll admit that his head's on right about kings and all, his whole notion to create a socialistic city in the heart of Texas is just plain stupid."

Gesturing toward the others who waited ahead of them in line, he said, "Look around you, lady. I'd lay odds not more than a dozen of these folks know the first little bit about farmin', much less what it takes for survivin' on the frontier. Take that crate, for instance." He shook his head incredulously, "They've stored work tools with violins for an ocean crossing, for goodness sake. These folks don't have the sense to pour rain water from a boot!" He popped the candy into his mouth, folded his arms across his chest, and studied the ship, chewing in a pensive silence.

The nerve of the man, Madeline thought, gritting her teeth against the words she'd love to speak. Really, to comment on another's intelligence when his own is so obviously lacking. Listen to his French.

And his powers of observation. Why, she knew how she looked.

Beautiful wasn't the appropriate word.

Brazos swallowed his candy and said, "Hmm. You've given me an idea." Before Madeline gathered her wits to stop him, he leaned over and kissed her cheek. "Thanks, Beauty. And listen, you take care out here without a man to protect you. If I see your husband on this boat I'm goin' to give him a piece of my mind about leavin' you alone." He winked and left her, walking toward the gangway.

Madeline touched the sticky spot on her cheek damp from his peppermint kiss and watched, fascinated despite herself, as the over-bold Texan tapped Considérant on the shoulder. In French that grated on her ears, he said. "Listen Frenchman, I'll make a deal with you. If you find a place for me on your ship I'll be happy to share my extensive knowledge of Texas with any of your folks who'd be interested in learnin'. This land you bought on the Trinity River—it's not more than half a day's ride from my cousin's spread. I've spent a good deal of time in that area over the past few years. I can tell you all about it."

"Mr. Sinclair," Considérant said in English, "please do not further abuse my language. I chose that land myself. Personally. I can answer any questions my peers may have about our new home. Now, as I have told you, this packet has been chartered to sail La Réunion colonists exclusively. Every space is assigned. I sympathize with your need to return to your home, but unfortunately the *Uriel* cannot accommodate you. Please excuse me, Monsieur Sinclair. I have much to see to before we sail. Good day."

"Good day my—" Brazos bit off his words. He turned abruptly and stomped away from the ship. Halting before Madeline, he declared, "This boat ain't leavin' until morning. It's not over yet. By General Taylor's tailor, when it sails, I'm gonna be on it."

He flashed a victorious grin and drawled, "Honey, you've captured my heart and about three other parts. I'll look forward to seein' you aboard ship."

As he walked away, she dropped a handsome gold pocket watch into her reticule, then called out to him in crisp, King's English. "Better you had offered your brain for ballast, Mr. Sinclair. Perhaps then you'd have been allowed aboard the *Uriel*."

And don't miss these spectacular
romances from Bantam Books,
on sale in December

DESIRE
by the nationally bestselling author
Amanda Quick

LONG TIME COMING
a classic romance by the
New York Times
bestselling author
Sandra Brown

STRANGER IN MY ARMS
a thrilling novel of romantic suspense
by **R. J. Kaiser**

WHERE DOLPHINS GO
by bestselling LOVESWEPT author
Peggy Webb
"Ms. Webb has an inventive mind brimming
with originality that makes all of her
books special reading."
—*Romantic Times*

And in hardcover from Doubleday

AMAZON LILY
by *Theresa Weir*
"Romantic adventure has no finer writer than
the spectacular Theresa Weir."
—*Romantic Times*

CALL JAN SPILLER'S ASTROLINE

DAILY PERSONALIZED PREDICTIONS!

ONLY FORECAST OF ITS KIND!

This is totally different from any horoscope you've ever heard and is the most authentic astrology forecast available by phone! Gain insight into LOVE, MONEY, HEALTH, WORK.

Empower yourself with this amazing astrology forecast. Let our intuitive tarot readings reveal with uncanny insight your personal destiny and the destinies of those close to you.

Jan Spiller, one of the world's leading authorities in astrological prediction, is an AFA Faculty Member, author, full-time astrologer, speaker at astrology and healing conferences, an astrology columnist for national newspapers and magazines, and had her own radio astrology show.

1-900-903-8000 ★ ASTROLOGY FORECAST
1-900-903-9000 ★ TAROT READING

99¢ For The First Min. ★ $1.75 For Each Add'l. Min. ★ Average Length Of Call 7 Min.

CALL NOW AND FIND OUT WHAT THE STARS HAVE IN STORE FOR YOU TODAY!

Call 24 hours a day, 7 days a week. You must be 18 years or older to call and have a touch tone phone. Astral Marketing 1-702-251-1415.

DHS 7/93

OFFICIAL RULES

To enter the sweepstakes below carefully follow all instructions found elsewhere in this offer.

The **Winners Classic** will award prizes with the following approximate maximum values: 1 Grand Prize: $26,500 (or $25,000 cash alternate); 1 First Prize: $3,000; 5 Second Prizes: $400 each; 35 Third Prizes: $100 each; 1,000 Fourth Prizes: $7.50 each. Total maximum retail value of Winners Classic Sweepstakes is $42,500. Some presentations of this sweepstakes may contain individual entry numbers corresponding to one or more of the aforementioned prize levels. To determine the Winners, individual entry numbers will first be compared with the winning numbers preselected by computer. For winning numbers not returned, prizes will be awarded in random drawings from among all eligible entries received. Prize choices may be offered at various levels. If a winner chooses an automobile prize, all license and registration fees, taxes, destination charges and, other expenses not offered herein are the responsibility of the winner. If a winner chooses a trip, travel must be complete within one year from the time the prize is awarded. Minors must be accompanied by an adult. Travel companion(s) must also sign release of liability. Trips are subject to space and departure availability. Certain black-out dates may apply.

The following applies to the sweepstakes named above:

No purchase necessary. You can also enter the sweepstakes by sending your name and address to: P.O. Box 508, Gibbstown, N.J. 08027. Mail each entry separately. Sweepstakes begins 6/1/93. Entries must be received by 12/30/94. Not responsible for lost, late, damaged, misdirected, illegible or postage due mail. Mechanically reproduced entries are not eligible. All entries become property of the sponsor and will not be returned.

Prize Selection/Validations: Selection of winners will be conducted no later than 5:00 PM on January 28, 1995, by an independent judging organization whose decisions are final. Random drawings will be held at 1211 Avenue of the Americas, New York, N.Y. 10036. Entrants need not be present to win. Odds of winning are determined by total number of entries received. Circulation of this sweepstakes is estimated not to exceed 200 million. All prizes are guaranteed to be awarded and delivered to winners. Winners will be notified by mail and may be required to complete an affidavit of eligibility and release of liability which must be returned within 14 days of date on notification or alternate winners will be selected in a random drawing. Any prize notification letter or any prize returned to a participating sponsor, Bantam Doubleday Dell Publishing Group, Inc., its participating divisions or subsidiaries, or the independent judging organization as undeliverable will be awarded to an alternate winner. Prizes are not transferable. No substitution for prizes except as offered or as may be necessary due to unavailability, in which case a prize of equal or greater value will be awarded. Prizes will be awarded approximately 90 days after the drawing. All taxes are the sole responsibility of the winners. Entry constitutes permission (except where prohibited by law) to use winners' names, hometowns, and likenesses for publicity purposes without further or other compensation. Prizes won by minors will be awarded in the name of parent or legal guardian.

Participation: Sweepstakes open to residents of the United States and Canada, except for the province of Quebec. Sweepstakes sponsored by Bantam Doubleday Dell Publishing Group, Inc., (BDD), 1540 Broadway, New York, NY 10036. Versions of this sweepstakes with different graphics and prize choices will be offered in conjunction with various solicitations or promotions by different subsidiaries and divisions of BDD. Where applicable, winners will have their choice of any prize offered at level won. Employees of BDD, its divisions, subsidiaries, advertising agencies, independent judging organization, and their immediate family members are not eligible.

Canadian residents, in order to win, must first correctly answer a time limited arithmetical skill testing question. Void in Puerto Rico, Quebec and wherever prohibited or restricted by law. Subject to all federal, state, local and provincial laws and regulations. For a list of major prize winners (available after 1/29/95): send a self-addressed, stamped envelope entirely separate from your entry to: Sweepstakes Winners, P.O. Box 517, Gibbstown, NJ 08027. Requests must be received by 12/30/94. DO NOT SEND ANY OTHER CORRESPONDENCE TO THIS P.O. BOX.

SWP 7/93

Don't miss these fabulous Bantam women's fiction titles

now on sale

• NOTORIOUS

by Patricia Potter, author of *RENEGADE*

Long ago, Catalina Hilliard had vowed never to give away her heart, but she hadn't counted on the spark of desire that flared between her and her business rival, Marsh Canton. Now that desire is about to spin Cat's carefully orchestrated life out of control.   ____56225-8 $5.50/6.50 in Canada

• PRINCESS OF THIEVES

by Katherine O'Neal, author of *THE LAST HIGHWAYMAN*

Mace Blackwood was a daring rogue—the greatest con artist in the world. Saranda Sherwin was a master thief who used her wits and wiles to make tough men weak. And when Saranda's latest charade leads to tragedy and sends her fleeing for her life, Mace is compelled to follow, no matter what the cost.

____56066-2 $5.50/$6.50 in Canada

• CAPTURE THE NIGHT

by Geralyn Dawson

In this "Once Upon a Time" Romance with "Beauty and the Beast" at its heart, Geralyn Dawson weaves the love story of a runaway beauty, the Texan who rescues her, and their precious stolen "Rose."   ____56176-6 $4.99/5.99 in Canada

---

Ask for these books at your local bookstore or use this page to order.

☐ Please send me the books I have checked above. I am enclosing $ _____ (add $2.50 to cover postage and handling). Send check or money order, no cash or C. O. D.'s please.

Name _____

Address _____

City/ State/ Zip _____

Send order to: Bantam Books, Dept. FN123, 2451 S. Wolf Rd., Des Plaines, IL 60018

Allow four to six weeks for delivery.

Prices and availability subject to change without notice.

FN123 12/93